Lo

by

Jade Winters

Lost In You

By Jade Winters

Published by Wicked Winters Books

WICKEDWINTERS

Copyright © 2017 Jade Winters

www.jade-winters.com

ISBN: 978-1-544-95180-5

Chapter One

Heidi sat deep in thought as the rain pelted against the windowpane of her sparsely-furnished office at the Young Minds Centre in Kentish Town. She was tired. Worn down by her lack of progress. Despite her tremendous effort in arranging fundraising events, donations were down again for the seventh month running. To her dismay, the public seemed to think that now being gay was 'tolerated', there was no longer the need to give money to organisations such as the one Heidi had managed for the past five years. But they couldn't have been more wrong. The teenagers that passed through the centre's doors each day were still vulnerable and looking for their place in the world. The social stigma of being a minority was a cause of anxiety and depression in itself. It was because of the services that places like Young Minds offered that troubled teenagers had the support to guide them through some of the darkest periods of their lives. It gave them hope.

It was an honour for Heidi to have been part of something that was so beneficial to so many people, which made her decision that much harder. On the computer screen in front of her was an online application form for a vacancy at Citizens Advice. She was applying for a debt advisor role, which seemed ironic considering the amount of debt she was in herself.

Fingers poised above the keyboard, Heidi began

typing and hastily entered her name, address and age. *Who'd have thought I'd be in this position at twenty-nine?* The younger Heidi had dreams and aspirations of owning her own home by the time she reached thirty, finally ready to settle down after travelling the world. Sadly, she'd achieved neither.

In which time frame do I plan to change jobs? Heidi paused. *Hmm, let me see … before I lose my home, perhaps?*

Resigned to the fact that leaving the centre was something that she had, no, needed to do, Heidi flew through the rest of the questions on the form. Once finished, she gave her answers a quick once over and hit the send button before she second-guessed herself.

A message box popped up announcing the successful transmission of the application.

Guilt crept into her mind but she pushed the thoughts aside swiftly. How could it be a bad thing for her to look for greener pastures so that she could keep a roof over her head?

The simple fact was that in the past year she had downsized in all areas of her life to keep debt at bay. She sold her car and bought a smaller one so she could cut back on fuel consumption. Meals out and takeaways were a no-no. All of the food she ate was cooked from scratch, the fruit and vegetables bought from the market. She couldn't even remember the last time she'd had a haircut. Yet at the end of each month, a week after payday, she was back into her overdraft again. It was a never-ending dilemma.

The silence in the room was broken by the shrill

sound of the phone ringing, jolting her from her ponderings. Heidi reached for the off-white device.

'YM,' she answered, abbreviating the name of the centre.

'Ms Cross?' a woman's voice asked.

'Speaking. How can I help you?'

'Hi there. This is Priscilla Jones, reporter from Channel Five News.'

What could a journalist want with me?

Before Heidi could hazard a guess, Priscilla continued, 'I'm calling to get your thoughts on the news. It must have been quite a shock for you.'

'And what news would that be?' Heidi asked, thinking she must be referring to another celebrity coming out of the closet. If that was the case, she had no comment at all.

'The announcement from Berkley O'Neil,' Priscilla informed her.

'Who the hell is he?'

'Who?' Priscilla asked.

Heidi furrowed her brows together and let out an exasperated breath, 'This man, Berkley, who—'

'Sorry, it's not a man, I'm referring to Berkley, O'Neil and Associates.' Priscilla paused for Heidi's reaction, but when she gave none Priscilla continued, 'The property developers?'

'I've never heard of them,' Heidi muttered.

'I'm surprised. I thought someone like you would know exactly who they are.'

What the hell is that supposed to mean? Like me? 'So

what's this big announcement you're going on about?'

'They've just bought your building—'

'They've done what? How—'

'It's what companies like that do. I suggest you look them up. In the meantime, can you tell me what this means for the charity? Will you have to close down?'

Close the centre down? Heidi's stomach churned over at the dire words, thinking of her colleagues losing their jobs, clients having nowhere to find solace. She looked out of the window up towards the clouds and wished she could somehow climb onto one and escape somewhere far, far away.

There were a few moments of silence before she spoke again. 'I know you're probably up against a deadline for your story, Priscilla, but I need time to speak to my staff before I make an official comment.'

'I'll be waiting for your call.'

Heidi dropped the receiver on its cradle. *Howard would have told us if he was selling up ... Wouldn't he?* Feeling horribly shaky, Heidi googled 'berkley o'neil property developers'. From what she could see on their homepage, the company developed luxury apartments for more money than she would earn in a lifetime. She tucked a stray strand of hair behind her ear as she scanned the page looking for an announcement of their latest purchase. Nothing. Heidi didn't know what to think. *Priscilla's got to be winding me up.* She gave a cynical laugh. *And to think I really believed her.*

For no reason other than curiosity, Heidi clicked

on the 'About Us' tab. *Craig O'Neil, CEO.* The photographer had captured a dark air of authority about him. Erect shoulders. A strong, forbidding jawline. The slight tilt of his chin gave the impression he was looking down on you. The look in his eyes was hard, callous even. Someone who didn't care who he trampled on to get his own way. Heidi knew she could be totally misjudging him, but for some reason she doubted it. *The eyes are the window to the soul, after all.*

Beneath his picture was ... Vanessa O'Neil. Heidi's mouth gaped open as the realisation of who she was dawned on her. The woman's face was forever in gay magazines and newspapers. Sleek and polished with long, thick, glossy hair falling in waves to her shoulders, framing her face which was both strong and beautiful. A smile curved her sensuous lips bringing warmth to her eyes that transfixed Heidi. *And a lot of other women too,* if her reputation was anything to go by. Vanessa was always photographed with a beautiful woman on her arm, but there had never been any mention of who she was actually dating. *Maybe she's like me and uses her job as the perfect cover for a shambolic love life.* In Heidi's not-so-extensive experience, finding a woman who was up for a bit of fun between the sheets was the easy part. It was forming a genuine connection outside of the bedroom that proved to be an uphill battle.

Heidi wasn't fussy by nature, on the contrary, the qualities she sought in a partner weren't outlandish in anyway. They were unassuming ones; compassionate, honest, warm, loving. Someone who could make her stomach flutter with butterflies with a simple glance. *Someone like Vanessa*. It was almost as if Heidi had somehow managed to conjure Vanessa O'Neil up out of her fantasies and made her a reality.

Heidi tutted, reigning herself in. The last thing she needed was to get hung up on a stranger on the internet, who the chances of meeting were zero to none.

Women like Vanessa—classy, rich, and sexy as hell—were well out of her league. Not only that, but Heidi wouldn't know how or where to meet such a woman. Just because they'd possibly bought the building didn't mean she'd show up at the centre, and it wasn't as if there was any chance of her bumping into Vanessa in the freezer aisle at her local Tesco.

With a slight shake of her head, Heidi forced the unattainable dream from her mind and turned her attention to the mounting paperwork piled on her desk. It needed to be tackled before it got much higher, but not until she took a quick peep at the property developer's Twitter page. *If they were going to announce anything big, surely it would be on there.* And if it wasn't? Then Priscilla Jones had played a cruel prank on her.

As the page loaded, goose pimples travelled the length of her arms and a twisting sensation in her stomach tightened like a snake around its prey, as she realised the reporter was spot on. Disbelief, shock and anger intermingled as her brain struggled to comprehend the words staring back at her.

Property acquired in Kentish Town. #Luxuryapartments.

Ten minutes earlier, Heidi would never have thought a two-word hashtag would be capable of stopping her world from spinning. Any form of hope seeped out of her completely as she dropped her face into her hands. *How can this be happening?*

Following the death of the previous landlord, Heidi assumed things would continue as normal, especially after the unexpected visit from his son, Howard. Now she realised what a naïve fool she'd been as she connected the dots.

Stupidly, she hadn't given Howard's surprise visit another thought. Nor had she suspected that something was going on—not even when his companion; a smug-faced woman, decked out in a black business suit, showed overzealous interest in the building. If she had thought for a second that Howard had been plotting the charity's demise right there in front of her, she would have … Heidi snorted. *I would have what? Begged, pleaded, grovelled? Yes, to all of the above, especially if it prevented the inevitable.*

Lost in her private reverie, Heidi jumped involuntarily as the door to her office burst open. The petite figure of a breathless Christina appeared at the entrance. At eighteen, she was one of the centre's youngest serving volunteers.

'Whoa, where's the fire?'

'Heidi, have you heard?' Christina didn't wait to be invited in. She crossed the room, tossing her shock of dark curly hair over her shoulder, and sagged down onto the chair opposite Heidi. A look of understanding was evident in her expressive blue eyes. 'You already know?'

Heidi gave a solemn nod.

'This place is going to be knocked down to erect a block of fucking flats.'

Christina was small in stature but her anger knew no bounds when confronted with injustice.

'Not just any old flats, Chris, luxury flats,' Heidi quipped, attempting to inject a little humour into the dire situation.

'I couldn't give a toss what they are. And do you know who runs the company? Vanessa O'Neil. A bloody lesbian! Turning her back on her own kind.'

The irony of it wasn't lost on Heidi. 'I didn't even realise she was a property developer. The last I heard she was some hot shot art dealer.'

Christina's shoulders slumped. Her eyes now brimmed with tears. 'They can't just evict us can they?'

'I'm going to have to look at the terms of the lease in detail, but from what I remember there is a break clause.'

'Which means?'

'Which means if the landlord decides to sell he can give us notice to leave.'

'You have to think of some way around it.' Christina looked pleadingly at her. 'Anything. We're all depending on you.'

The last thing Heidi needed was Christina laying the huge responsibility of saving the centre on shoulders, especially in the midst of her own soon-to-be-homeless drama. A small groan escaped her lips. Yes, in the past, Heidi had taken on the opposition and won, but they were nerdy civil servants giving her a hard time over her request for bigger recycling bins. Civil servants were not in the same league as property developers— rich property developers with extremely deep pockets at that.

In life there were winners and losers, and Heidi knew that Young Minds were going to be the latter. Instead of saying this aloud, Heidi slumped back in her seat. Even though, *touch wood*, she might not be the manager for much longer, it pained her greatly to think of the centre closing. She wanted it to thrive. To have new life breathed into it for the next generations of gay teenagers.

This last thought made something inside her stir with indignation. *What the hell am I thinking? Me, abandon a sinking ship when I'm needed most. Never! So what if I'm made homeless before I get another job? If I can save the centre, I'll always have my office to sleep in.*

Heidi needed to pull on her big-girl pants and put aside her own personal needs until the centre was safe. She would do whatever she had to in order to achieve her goal. Local councillors had always applauded the charity for the outstanding service they provided and with this knowledge in her armoury, Heidi concluded she needed a plan of attack to outsmart the developers. Kick up a public storm. Get local people behind them. And she knew exactly how to do that.

Adrenaline seeped into her veins as she rose from her chair. 'Christina, contact the local newspapers and

TV stations. I'm going to give a press conference.'

Not only did Christina's face light up, but so did Heidi's heart.

'A press conference!' Christina clasped her hands in excitement. 'When and where? Do you want me to arrange it for Thursday?'

Heidi shook her head so ferociously that her hair whipped across her cheeks. 'Thursday will be too late. It has to be tomorrow. At ten. We'll meet the media in front of the building, so our banners can be seen on camera.'

Heidi would fight this eviction to the bitter end because she was proud of what the charity stood for and, more than that, it was her job.

Chapter Two

Vanessa sat behind her desk on the 12th floor of Berkley, O'Neil and Associates in central London. The company's long serving chief architect, Brett Jenkins, sat opposite and their attention was focused on a large sheet plan. The mild rumble of thunder outside resembled a drum beat, running from one side of the room to the other, but soon came another sort of thunder—her brother, Craig.

He burst through her office door without so much as a knock, because, as Vanessa knew, Craig had never met courtesy or its distant cousin, consideration. With his blue suit jacket flapping in flight, he all but shouted, 'Vanessa.'

Vanessa looked up from the plan. 'Craig, you can see I'm busy. I'll come to your office when I'm done.'

Craig ignored her. 'Brett, out. Now. Vanessa, this is urgent.' Craig made for the flat screen TV in her makeshift waiting area. He threw himself over the sofa, sidestepped the coffee table and grabbed the TV remote.

Vanessa rose from her seat and said through gritted teeth, 'What the hell are you doing? Do you really think I've got time to watch TV?'

After their father suffered a heart attack and could no longer work, Craig had appointed himself patriarch of the family. This meant he thought he could still pull rank over her, like when they were kids. Even adulthood didn't absolve her from Craig punishing, no, bullying her. He ignored the fact that she was a grown woman of thirty and still treated her as if she was a little brat under his trampling feet.

Brett stood and moved towards the door. 'I'll catch up with you later, Vanessa.'

Vanessa gave him an apologetic glance. 'I won't be long.'

'Yes you will.' The TV screen filled with a news segment showing a group of protesters outside a residential building. 'Sit,' he ordered.

Vanessa dropped back into her chair as the energy sapped from her and wearily said, 'What's this about, Craig?'

'Remember that building we bought in Kentish Town?'

'The red brick mews?'

'No, no, no. That property next to the park.'

'The three-story with the garden?' she asked, remembering the proposals for a building he'd shoved under her nose while she was driving.

'Yeah that one. Now get this. The owner …. No, not owner, the manager of the charity housed there has a bone to pick with us about it.' He slapped his thigh in delight. 'Fancies herself a hero of the people or something. I'll show her—'

'You can be such an arsehole sometimes.'

'Sometimes? Most of the time,' he boasted, beaming through his reddened face and growing double chin. He loosened his tie as if the news would be an event to watch.

A painfully thin newscaster with her hair tied in a ponytail graced the screen. Her flawless skin and impeccably made-up face stared back at them as her cultured, even-toned voice filled the room.

'Today, Heidi Cross, manager at the Young Minds Centre, called a press conference to address the Berkley O'Neil purchase of the building in which the counselling centre is housed. Tim Holmes spoke to Heidi Cross from the centre and now reports.'

'Can you believe it? She just wants to get her face on TV to bitch about the inevitable. This is what happens when people don't want to accept change. They become bitter and twisted.'

Vanessa tuned out Craig's rantings. The only thing that now held her attention was the attractive woman on the high-definition screen. She looked calm and composed as she spoke.

'Needless to say, we at Young Minds are devastated by our impending eviction after Berkley O'Neil thought it was a good idea to add our charity building to their already rocketing property development business. By doing this, they are taking away one of the only places where gay teenagers and young adults can come for help. These young people need us. They need to know that they are more important than some corporation's bank account. That's why I'm speaking out and bringing our plight to the public. I believe our clients are more important than a block of luxury flats and I'm sure anyone with a heart will agree.'

Heidi's voice caused Vanessa's skin to tingle, as if she were slowly caressing her body with the tip of her tongue.

It takes a special kind of heartless money-monger to close down a place like our centre for their own unnecessary gain. They would never dare show their faces and come and see for themselves what a difference the centre makes in people's lives every day. This is not just a building; it is a hub of life and gives hope to the users of the service we provide. In fact,' Heidi stared directly into the camera as if she were personally addressing Vanessa herself. *'I invite the owners at Berkley, O'Neil and Associates to visit us for just one day.'*

Vanessa's stomach flipped over as her gaze remained glued to the screen. Her attraction to Heidi was not just because she was a natural, down-to-earth beauty with stunning red hair and green come-to-bed eyes. She was also intensely drawn to her fiery attitude. Heidi Cross exhibited a warring spirit but still appeared compassionate and rational. All the qualities Vanessa admired in a woman.

'Does she really think that little speech is going to make us change our minds?' Craig said with the faintest touch of ridicule in his voice as he switched the TV off.

'Craig, you didn't say anything about turfing a charity out of the building.'

'Who gives a toss. It's just a building.'

'That just happens to counsel vulnerable gay people. How is that going to make me look once they associate me with the eviction?'

'Not my problem.' He snorted. 'You sound as whiney as that bloody manager.'

Vanessa shook her head in dismay at Craig's

reaction to her obvious dilemma. Added to that, he just didn't see what she saw in Heidi. All he sensed was a fight, and he was gunning for it.

'Not only is she making a complete idiot of herself in public by challenging us, she thinks that provoking us will get our attention. It's a shame such a pretty thing is so desperate.' He gestured to his crotch area and let out a lascivious laugh. 'Of course, if she wants my attention, I'd be happy to give her a good once-over at one of our apartments—on the house of course.'

'Do you have to be so vile?' Vanessa said. 'And regardless of what you think, she doesn't strike me as someone who's going down without a fight. In fact, I think you might have met your match.'

Craig's face changed to a serious display of irritation. Heidi Cross had clearly got under his skin, regardless of the brave charade he displayed. He sat quietly for a while, his eyes darting from side to side as his brain worked overtime. Then he snapped his head towards her.

'Vanessa, you know the value of this deal. I'm not going to let one loser backed by a bunch of ...' Vanessa raised her eyebrows '... Unruly gay people derail the process.'

Vanessa couldn't help but think of the upheaval an eviction would cause to the people who used the charity's services *and the damage to my reputation.* She doubted she could change Craig's mind but it was worth a try. She gave him a tight-lipped smile. 'Why don't you see if you can come to a compromise?'

Craig looked at her as if he wanted to skewer her alive. His face shifted from confusion to anger. 'Wait. You're not seriously considering this fucking challenge, are you? Are you out of your mind? You want me to give in to some whiney bitc—woman and compromise this company's integrity and … and power?'

Vanessa shrugged. 'It's up to you. But remember, if she pulls another public stunt like that one, we might have the council telling us to rethink our plans.'

Craig's features instantly softened and he even gestured with his head that he was listening to a voice of reason. Vanessa continued, 'The public will believe everything she said and think we're cowards hiding in the shadows. That we bully vulnerable people for the sake of profits.'

Craig opened his mouth to argue, then promptly closed it when she raised her hand.

'Do you want to prove her right, just because your over-inflated ego can't bear to be wrong?'

Craig jumped up from the sofa, walked over to her desk and stared her down with contempt. 'It sickens me how someone of your wealth and success would give a shit what the public and that pathetic bitch think of us.'

Vanessa recoiled when Craig slammed his right hand on the desk.

'You're a disgrace to this family. Weak, girly and stupid. There's no place in this business for a do-gooder like you. Why don't you step the fuck aside and let the big boys run the show?'

Sweat beaded on his top lip and Vanessa wondered

just how much self-control it took for him not to strike her. She remained silent under his taunting eyes, not wanting to provoke him any further. Craig stormed towards the door, shaking his head while mumbling about what a waste of space she was. He cast her one last hateful glare before he jerked the door wide open and slammed it shut behind him.

No matter how hard he tried he could never hide his resentment that their parents had given Vanessa equal shares in the company. To their credit, they had known Craig was not the kind of man that should hold excessive power over anyone or anything. Before they retired to Florida, their parents had always kept Craig in check, but unfortunately they weren't around anymore to maintain that balance. He was out of control in his quest to build a property empire in London and its surrounding areas.

If Vanessa hadn't given up running her own successful art business to save their father's legacy before Craig destroyed it, she would have left him to get on with it, but that wasn't even an option now. She had too much to lose so she had to at least try and minimise any potential damage Craig might cause. Engaging in a dispute with a charity was not the sort of fight she wanted played out in the public domain.

Heidi. The woman haunted her mind on so many levels.

She reached for the phone and connected with her secretary. 'Gina, get hold of Priscilla Jones at Channel Five News. Tell her I want to respond to the comments

Heidi Cross made today.'

Not only would Vanessa save their company's reputation by putting a positive spin on the purchase of the charity's building, but Craig would be livid with her for speaking in public about it. *A double score for me.*

She smiled as she looked at the black screen that had so recently held the image of Heidi's arresting face.

Chapter Three

Why do adults lie? Kelli pondered. *They make statements as if they were set in stone: 'Don't worry about it', 'You'll soon get over it', 'Everything will be all right'.* What exactly did these words mean to someone whose whole world had caved in? Jack shit was what they meant. As far as she was concerned, adults could stick their 'I know best' platitudes up their arses. They were a bunch of losers with their smarmy smiles, patronising voices and fake promises of better things to come. *Well guess what? Nothing ever got better. If anything, they just got worse.*

Kelli looked down at her mother's gravestone. Lauren O'Neil. 1979 – 2016.

Tears welled in her eyes at the thought of her mum being buried under six feet of mud, worms and insects. At sixteen, she was on the cusp of adulthood, the grey area in-between, so crying was the last thing she should be doing. Society dictated that she should be able to cope with her emotions by now. *If only it were that easy.* Her mum had been everything to her and now she was gone. Kelli had no one—well, no one who genuinely cared. Her aunt Vanessa tried to put on a good show about being there for her but work always came first. From the minute she woke up, Vanessa's head was stuck in a newspaper or her iPad, then she'd leave the house and wouldn't return until she thought Kelli was asleep. The last time Kelli checked, looking after someone involved more than putting a roof over their head, but that was all her aunt had done for her.

Kelli's mobile phone beeped. Without thinking, she removed it from her pocket but didn't check the messages straight away. She knew who it was from. Jason: the one boy all the girls lusted over at college, but who, for some reason, was only interested in Kelli. She gave it a few minutes before she unlocked her phone. When she did, her heartbeat pounded in her chest, making it nearly impossible for her to breathe as she read and re-read the words over and over.

I know why you don't want me.

What does he know? He can't have found out the truth. Kelli momentarily forgot about her mum and she quickly tapped a response:

What's that supposed to mean?

She waited. Every second that ticked by seemed like an hour. When he still hadn't replied five minutes later, her panic level elevated to red. Kelli paced the gravel floor. Four steps forward, an abrupt turn, four paces back. Her hands trembled as she checked and re-checked her phone.

'Come on, Jason. Answer me for fuck's sake.' Her voice quivered. 'Bloody answer me.'

A passer-by stared at her with suspicion and hurried past with a bunch of flowers held tightly against her chest. Kelli attempted to give her a reassuring look, but it didn't work. The woman bowed her head and quickened her pace.

'Oh piss off then,' Kelli muttered under her breath.

She probably believes all the shit she reads in the papers about teenagers being the new terrorists.

Kelli turned her attention back to her phone. It beeped. She inhaled deeply, prepared for the worst.

You know exactly what it means. You've been keeping secrets.

Kelli's legs buckled beneath her and she used the headstone to keep herself upright. With her free hand, she smacked her forehead hard. 'No, no, no, no, he can't know.'

Kelli's breath rasped in her throat and her thoughts were muddled as she tried to figure out how to respond. Before she got the chance, her phone beeped again. Even though she dreaded seeing the words in black and white, she couldn't help but look.

Evan told me that you wanted to shag him.

Evan? She laughed out loud as she looked heavenward. 'Thank you, God,' she said, more out of habit than in the true belief that a grey-haired man in the sky was looking over her. *Trust Evan to save the day with his wild fantasies.*

That was one text message she wouldn't be

responding to. Best to leave Jason with the image of her being a slut than him finding out the truth.

Kelli bent down, kissed her mother's headstone and promised to visit her next week, before heading towards the exit. As she walked, Kelli thought about all the things that could go wrong if anyone found out about her secret. Not only would she have the piss taken out of her on a daily basis, but the news could also get back to her aunt. She didn't particularly like lying but it was the only choice she had. Not that it really mattered. That was another thing adults told lies about: that you should always tell the truth.

It was funny how the ones who surrounded her did anything but.

Chapter Four

Heidi's sister always gave it to her straight and today was no exception. Sat at the dining table in their parents' homely kitchen, Amanda stared at Heidi despairingly. 'Wake up! This is not your battle to fight. You're a stone's throw away from being kicked out of your flat and you think you've got time to act like a martyr?'

'The centre needs me—'

'And you need some sense knocked into you. What's it going to take? For you to get home from work one day and find your stuff out on the street?'

Heidi frowned and pouted. 'Come on, it's not that bad.'

'Isn't it? You eat value food from Tesco for God's sake—'

'That's my choice,' Heidi said, wishing she'd never brought the subject of the centre up. If she could only wind back the clock a few minutes, they could be engrossed in a conversation that wasn't so emotive, like the weather.

'I give up,' Amanda said in the authoritarian voice she used when she wanted to shut Heidi down, which was most of the time as they barely agreed on anything. 'You never listen to what I say anyway.'

'That's not true. I applied for the job at Citizens Advice didn't I? And anyway, I didn't say I wasn't going to leave the centre—'

'But you didn't say when you will.'

'Because I can't—'

Amanda raised her eyebrows. 'Or won't?'

'I will. But just not right now.'

'You two ....' Tess, their mother, intervened brightly as she stirred a pan of baked beans on the hob. 'Stop bickering.'

Amanda's surly expression dissolved into a smile. 'We're not bickering. Heidi is just being her usual stubborn self.'

Heidi clasped her hands together under the table. They were safer there than wrapped around Amanda's neck. *She's so infuriating.*

'Are you at least going to tell the centre you're leaving?' Tess opened the oven to check the browning sausages and it released a mouth-watering aroma that exacerbated Heidi's hunger pangs.

'Not you as well, Mum. I came here for breakfast, not an inquisition.'

'What did I do? I only asked a question.' Tess rolled her eyes as she took the tray out of the oven and slammed the door shut. Jamming a fork into a sausage she held it in the air. 'One or two?'

'Two please,' Heidi said.

'In that case I'll have one,' Amanda said. 'I have to watch my weight, unlike some people.'

Heidi poked out her tongue. It wasn't her fault she could eat anything and not gain weight. Yet with the passive-aggressive comments Amanda made, anyone would think Heidi was only slim to spite her.

'I think you did the right thing making the centre's troubles public. It might not get you anywhere, but at least you're not taking it lying down,' Tess said, dishing out the food before handing them each a plate. She retrieved her own plate from the worktop and joined her daughters at the table. 'The least the developers could have done was give you some notice.'

'They have now. Two months wasn't it?' Amanda said with a smirk.

'Whose side are you on anyway?' Heidi shot back.

'Yours, Heidi, if you—'

'Yeah, I know, I know. If I hadn't dropped out of medical school, I wouldn't be in the mess I'm in now. Seriously, Mandy, you're starting to sound like a broken record.'

Tess took a mouthful of food and chewed thoughtfully. 'Your sister does have a point ....'

'Oh, Mum, give me a break. I thought you supported me on my decision to quit.'

'I did and I do,' Tess said quickly, giving Heidi's hand a squeeze, 'But looking at how your life has turned out. Maybe I should have encouraged you to finish.'

Heidi stared at Tess. Had she forgotten the severe anxiety Heidi had suffered? Did she not remember the times where Heidi would be so stressed out with her workload that she couldn't sleep for days?

'So you're saying you'd rather have a rich but thoroughly depressed daughter? How would that have been any better than the situation I'm in now?'

'You know what they say, better to be rich and

miserable than poor and miserable,' Amanda said sitting back with a smile of triumph.

Heidi glanced at her but said nothing. Five years older and a doctor herself, Amanda wasn't exactly the poster girl for happiness. This was the third week in as many months that Amanda had retreated to their parents' home for a so-called 'break'. Her sister had invented a world of make-believe where everything in her marriage to Ellis Fallon was perfect. Heidi might have bought into her fairy tale had she not overheard Amanda talking to Ellis on the phone. She'd been shocked to hear Amanda tell him in no uncertain terms that she was miserable with her life and being married to him was only making things worse.

Amanda would never admit to failing at anything. Ever. Her sister would rather die than admit to the true state of her marriage, even to her own family. In order to spare Amanda any embarrassment, Heidi did what any loving sister would do—she colluded in Amanda's falsehood and nodded in agreement when she pointed out that one day Heidi could be as lucky as her and find the partner of her dreams.

'But you are though, aren't you?' Tess was saying. 'Unhappy I mean. All you do is work and if you're not working you're at home moping around.'

'Only because I'm knackered. It's stressful dealing with problems all day.'

Not that the stress at work was unbearable. It wasn't. All Heidi meant was that when she got home she liked to switch off and chill out by reading or taking a candlelit bath. Enjoying having time to herself was hardly 'moping about' as her mum had so kindly put it.

Nevertheless, Tess and Amanda's silence spoke volumes, which only served to raise Heidi's defences even higher.

'I love my job,' Heidi directed her statement at Amanda. 'I really do. And I swear I don't have any regrets about my career choices.'

'But?' Amanda said.

The gold glinted mirror on the wall opposite gave Heidi the reflection of a weary woman. Worry and woe shaded her eyes and pulled at the corners of her mouth. She looked exactly how she felt. Exhausted and at the end of her tether.

'There aren't any buts,' Heidi protested half-heartedly.

'If you say so.' Amanda sliced her sausage with precision and popped a piece in her mouth.

'I'm starting to wish I'd gone straight to work instead of coming here.'

'Don't be such a baby,' Tess said, 'We're just making small talk.'

'It sounds like badgering to me,' Heidi said, feeling her blood pressure start to rise.

'So what is it you're looking for exactly? Advice?' Amanda asked dabbing her mouth with a napkin before putting it on her now empty plate.

'If it's sensible, yes,' Heidi said. *Starting with how to find another office space that accepted peanuts in lieu of rent.* Because that's about all the charity could afford. Next would be how to find the right words to tell her colleagues she was planning to leave once all the drama was over.

It had been three days and she still hadn't worked up the nerve to tell anyone that she'd been called in for an interview. Under normal circumstances, she would have gone straight to Simone to share the good news. *Right about now she'd be telling me what not to wear and how I should do my hair.*

But these were not normal circumstances. If news of her seeking employment elsewhere came out while everyone was embroiled in the all-encompassing task of saving the centre, it would be catastrophic. There was no doubt in her mind that her colleagues, volunteers, and clients would perceive her as a traitor. A coward, who was abandoning them in their hour of need.

'Okay, here's what I'd do if I was in your position,' Amanda said switching to her proactive mode. 'I would talk directly to your new landlords. There's no point keep airing your grievances on TV. Too impersonal. Besides, they might not have even seen your interview.'

That thought hadn't even occurred to Heidi but it actually made sense. She felt a renewed surge of excitement. 'You're right—the only contact we've had from them was the letter giving us notice.'

'Exactly. But whatever you do, don't get in their face about it. State your case fact by fact—'

'I know exactly what to say.' Heidi pulled her hair back in a ponytail, leaving it unkempt as it twirled to her collarbone. She looked across the table at Amanda.

'When are you going home?'

'In a few days.'

'I'll drop by before you go. Sorry I can't finish breakfast, Mum.' Heidi grabbed a sausage and stuffed it halfway into her mouth. 'Tell Dad I love him. Call you both later.'

Heidi grabbed her jacket from the back of her chair and headed out the door. *I'm such an idiot,* she chided herself as she hurried to the bus stop. Amanda was right of course. Before shouting her mouth off in public she should have made her case with the developers in private. *And let that be a lesson. Think before you act next time!*

With every minute that passed, Heidi became more and more nervous at the thought of coming face-to-face with Vanessa and being ... What? *Rejected? Humiliated?* Or simply just mesmerised?

***

Finding the Berkley O'Neil office building was easy enough. Situated in Central London, the office block stood tall and proud. While the buildings on either side were in a run-down condition with peeling paint and dirty windows, Berkley O'Neil's towering glass building glistened in the sunlight like a giant diamond.

But what wasn't easy, as Heidi was about to find out, was getting in front of Vanessa to plead her case. A middle-aged woman was seated behind a desk in a large reception area engrossed in her computer screen. She didn't look up until Heidi stood in front of her and cleared her throat.

'I'd like to see Vanessa O'Neil please.'

Beady brown eyes bored into hers. 'Do you have an appointment?'

Heidi shook her head.

'Then you'll have to make one.'

'Fine. Pencil me in please, Liz,' Heidi added reading the name tag on her blouse which strained against her large breasts.

Liz tapped a few keys on the keyboard. 'Let's see. The earliest I can fit you in will be the 23rd—'

'Brilliant.' Today was the 21st. Heidi could cope with waiting another two days if it meant getting her argument across. On the plus side, it would give her time to put together a reasonable proposal. 'I can wait a couple of days if I have to.'

Liz frowned. 'I meant the 21st of May.'

'What? Are you kidding? We're in March.'

'I'm sorry but Ms O'Neil is a very busy woman.'

'It's going to be too late. Look is there any way you can help me out. It's urgent. We're going to be evicted—'

'I do sympathise with you Ms Cross—'

'Wait, you know who I am?'

'Of course.' Liz pointed at the large flat screen TV mounted on the wall. 'I saw your interview the other day.'

'So you can understand why I need to see her?'

'Like I said, Ms O'Neil is very busy.' Liz leant

forward and whispered in a conspiratorial tone, 'In fact, she'll be leaving the building for an appointment in a few minutes.'

'Uh? That's no good ....' It took a few seconds for it to dawn on her that Liz was indirectly helping her. 'Ah, I see. Thank you.'

'No, thank you for looking out for those kids.'

The lift doors pinged and opened in the corridor behind the reception desk. Heidi glanced up past Liz, as a group of smartly dressed people talking animatedly emerged. Three men and Vanessa O'Neil. She looked every inch the business woman, dressed in a pinstriped black suit that accentuated her figure in all the right places.

Startled by Vanessa's sudden appearance, Heidi's brain froze. It took Liz's whisper of urgency for it to defrost. 'Here's your chance.'

Mmm. She looks so much better in the flesh. Heidi licked her bottom lip, then said in a trance like voice. 'It's really her isn't it?'

'Yes and you've got about thirty seconds to catch her. So get moving.'

Heart in her mouth, Heidi waited until Vanessa and her colleagues walked through into the foyer. Struggling to find her voice, Heidi waved her hand in the air to gain Vanessa's attention. It was in vain. Vanessa was engrossed in deep conversation with a tall, slender, dark-haired man who held a thick folder in one hand.

Come on, Heidi, remember, victory favours the brave. It

was the self-motivator she needed. 'Ms O'Neil?' she called out.

No response. Vanessa was near the exit. A few more steps and she would be outside and no doubt whisked away in her private car. Heidi advanced quicker in her direction.

'Ms O'Neil?' Heidi called again only louder this time.

Vanessa stopped and turned.

A charge of electricity slammed into Heidi's body. She tugged at the base of her top thinking that was the reason her breathing had become shallow. *She's amazing. I can't believe I'm actually breathing the same air as her. In the same space.*

Heidi neared. Standing only feet away, their gaze locked. *Grey eyes. Gorgeous, stormy grey eyes.* The eyeliner Vanessa wore only highlighted them, giving them an unsettling, staring quality. It felt as if Vanessa's eyes were piercing her soul.

Heidi's gaze dropped to Vanessa's chest and the way in which her hair brushed gently against her cleavage. The mere sight of this made her giddy with excitement.

Vanessa gave her a quizzical look. 'Can I help you?'

'I … I'm…' *You're so much more than what I imagined.* 'I'm Heidi Cross, from Young Minds. Your company just—'

Vanessa squared her shoulders in a defensive pose. 'Bought your premises. Yes, I know.'

Heidi was waiting for an 'and?' but Vanessa said no more.

'Yes, about that. I was wondering if we could sit down and talk?'

'Make an appointment—'

'I just tried. You're booked up for two months solid.' Heidi attempted a light-hearted laugh. 'Please. If I could just have two minutes of your time.'

'Time is one thing I don't have,' Vanessa said as if Heidi's needs were inconsequential.

Heidi's forehead wrinkled slightly at the chill in Vanessa's voice. The unexpectedly cold reception was all it took to obliterate any silly romantic notions she had about Vanessa. Heidi wondered if she should just leave but rejected the idea immediately.

Why the hell am I being so nice to her? She's the one responsible for evicting us from the centre and by the looks of it, doesn't give a damn either. Heidi's temples pounded, her throat tightened. When she spoke again she could barely keep the contempt out of her voice. 'No, people like you don't have a lot of time, do they? Especially for those who you don't give a shit about.'

Vanessa fixed her with a challenging, pissed off stare. 'Ms Cross—'

'How the hell do people like you manage to sleep at night?' *The last thing I need to be thinking about is her in bed.* 'Do you count how much money you've made in a day instead of sheep? Do you give a single thought about the lives you ruin with—'

A middle-aged, short, stocky man stepped protectively in front of Vanessa. 'That's enough. You need to leave this building right now.'

Heidi sidestepped him. 'That's about right. There's always someone to do your dirty work for you, isn't there?'

Vanessa touched the man's arm and he reluctantly moved to the side. 'I have my day ahead planned—'

'Plans? Funnily enough, we had plans as well—until you lot decided to evict us.'

'Are you going to let me speak?'

'Are you going to talk about the injustice of what you're doing to us?'

Vanessa raised her eyebrows. 'Do you really think this is the best way to get my attention? First by publicly shaming us and now—'

'How about you try and put yourself in the shoes of the little people for once. How would *you* have gone about getting your attention?'

'Not like this,' Vanessa said.

The dark-haired man tapped his watch and Vanessa gave a slight nod. The man then beckoned a security guard who was talking into his walkie-talkie. 'Times up.' His voice was final.

'Don't worry. I'm going. To think I thought it was your brother who looked like a hard-faced bastard. He's got nothing on you, has he?' Heidi said, as a last parting shot to Vanessa. It was time to retreat before the no-nonsense security man got hold of her.

What a bitch! I can't believe it. Just goes to show that beauty accounts for nothing.

From the bus stop opposite the building, Heidi watched Vanessa and her entourage approach a waiting car. Before Vanessa climbed in, she stopped as if sensing Heidi's stare, and looked straight in her direction. Heidi couldn't see the expression on her face. *One of contempt I bet.* Then Vanessa ducked inside and the car sped off.

By now Heidi had composed herself. *And that is how not to approach someone when you need their help.* Heidi boarded the bus and sat at the front. *What a fucking disaster. How am I going to explain to Simone and the team that I have made things even worse?*

During the twenty-minute journey to work, Heidi replayed the scenario in her head. Why had she lost her cool? Amanda had warned her not to 'get in their face' but that's exactly what she had done. The regret of acting on impulse grew deeper by the second and no amount of self-loathing satisfied her conscience.

Like her Dad used to say, 'That temper of yours will be the ruin of you one day', and Heidi knew that day had finally come.

***

Heidi's skin prickled and sweat formed between her breasts as she arrived at work to find a small group of people standing outside the entrance. Heidi recognised them as the parents of some of her clients. A wave of panic washed over her. *Shit, shit, shit! What am I going to tell them?*

'Heidi, is it true? Is the centre going to close?' asked a concerned Mum as Heidi neared.

'Nothing's set in stone, Debs,' Heidi answered as confidently as she could.

Her management training had tempered her against showing tension. Only now for the first time did she realise how strenuous and difficult it was to keep everyone stable and assured.

'When will you be seeing the new owners?' another woman asked.

Heidi pulled the glass door open and stopped halfway inside. 'I've … Um, I'm working hard to try and find a solution—'

'But where will our kids go for help if you can't find one? How do I keep Micky from self-harming without this place? He's just starting to get on his feet,' one of the fathers implored in a quivering voice that broke Heidi's heart.

'Please try not to worry.' *Not yet anyway.* 'We'll work something out. These property moguls are people, just like us. They have families too. I'm sure they'll understand our dilemma,' she said before she disappeared inside.

Privately, Heidi knew her words were futile. Sadly, after her encounter with Vanessa, she also knew there was little or no chance of getting her to change her mind now.

Heidi bypassed her office and walked straight to the kitchenette for a much-needed caffeine hit. As she entered, the expression on Simone's face told her all she needed to know: she should brace herself for another difficult day. But Heidi knew the situation couldn't get much worse—not now anyway.

'Morning,' Heidi said to no one in particular as she made for the kettle.

'Any news yet?' Christina asked, taking a sip from her mug.

Heidi answered her question with a question. 'Who's in today?'

'Um, let's see. Richie, Harry, Mel and Kirsty.'

'Okay that'll be enough. Would you get everyone together in the conference room please. I'm at a dead-end so we need to brainstorm and see if we can come up with a new plan of action.' *Since mine seem to fail miserably.*

Christina nodded, placed her almost untouched coffee on the worktop and left.

'Wow, you look like shit,' Simone said, slinking up beside her.

'Thanks.'

'No, I'm serious. Have you been sleeping?'

Heidi pulled a face. 'Do you really need to ask?'

'Suppose not.'

'Oh, Sim, you're gonna kill me. I think I've really put my foot in it.' Heidi poured boiling water into her cup and stirred.

Simone playfully nudged Heidi's shoulder, 'You been up to something naughty?'

'I wish it were that simple.' She bowed her head. 'I went to see Vanessa O'Neil.'

Simone's eyes widened. 'And?'

'And …' Heidi let out a long breath. 'I fucked up big time.'

'No!' Simone gasped. 'How? What did you do?'

'I lost my rag. I can't believe that under the circumstances she couldn't even give me two minutes of her precious time. I don't know why but I thought she was different.'

'Because she's gay? I wouldn't worry about it,' Simone said in a determined tone that Heidi had never heard her use before. 'You'll figure a way around this. If anyone can get us out of this mess, it's you.'

Great. Nothing like being reminded that the future of the centre is my responsibility.

Ten minutes later, Heidi walked nervously into the conference room. Why she was apprehensive she didn't know. These people were her friends. They had been through hell and back together, but reminding herself of this did nothing to alleviate the heaviness she felt as she sat down at the head of the table and took in the expectant faces turned towards her.

'Right, let's get started,' Heidi took a quick sip of coffee and put her cup on the table. 'As you may have noticed, my interview with the press failed to get the reaction I'd hoped for. So I … I went to see Vanessa O'Neil this morning—'

'What did she have to say for herself?' Mel interrupted.

'Nothing much, she didn't have time to talk. She was in a rush.' That was true, Vanessa hadn't said much. Her face was still imprinted on Heidi's mind—only now there was a burning resentment when she thought about her, not a lovey-dovey crush.

'You should have asked her why it's so important for them to occupy this space when there are other areas in London they can develop,' Christina butted in.

'And why isn't there more of a public outcry?' Mel looked pained. 'People are too busy with their heads stuck in virtual realities to even notice what's going on around them.'

'We need to force them to meet with us,' Christina said.

'Yeah, like that's gonna happen. Didn't you hear what Heidi said?' Richie narrowed his eyes. 'Rich people don't have time for lowlifes like us.'

'So if we don't move out within two months, what will they do to us?' Kirsty asked.

'They'll probably put one of those huge unpickable padlocks on the front door,' Simone said.

Heidi took a deep breath and let it out slowly. 'I'm beginning to think I should have never gone to the press with this. I might have rubbed them up the wrong way by calling them out in public.' *And by showing up unannounced at Vanessa's office and being mega rude.*

'Don't blame yourself. They left us no choice.' Harry gave her a reassuring smile. 'We had to find out they bought the place through a third party. They're the ones in the wrong.'

'Well, there's no point going round in circles,' Heidi said with finality. 'Whether they're the bad guys or not, they are legally within their rights to evict us. What we need to do is focus on what we can do to get out of this mess.'

'We could always start a petition?' Kirsty said. She had only been working at the centre for a month, tirelessly manning the phones each evening.

'What, like the one that tried to get a second vote for Brexit?' Richie replied. 'Those things are a waste of time and energy.'

'In that case we might as well start packing today,' Mel said miserably.

'How about we picket their building? I'm sure they won't like having us in their face day in, day out until one of their lot talk to us,' Harry suggested in his usual shrill voice. He was an excellent counsellor and appeared to be a decade younger than he was. He dressed with casual flair and knew all the trending styles and music, which made him popular with the teenagers he counselled.

'Hey, that's not a bad idea, Harry,' Simone said.

Heidi reached across the table to grab a chocolate biscuit from the plate.

'Bang goes the diet,' Simone said, grinning.

Heidi returned her smile as she nibbled on the biscuit. 'Protesting outside their offices could be something to think about I suppose. I'm just worried it will have the opposite effect. If we really piss them off there'll be no comeback for us.' *And no doubt security would be quick to move us on.*

'So what do we do?' Mel asked.

In her heart, Heidi knew their fate. She had tasted defeat in her mouth the minute her eyes met Vanessa's. When she wasn't drowning in them that is.

It was time for Heidi to lay her cards on the table. 'I think we need to face reality. We either find new premises or—'

'—Or?' The group said in unison.

'Or …' Heidi's voice broke with emotion. 'We admit defeat and … and close the centre down.'

Chapter Five

Vanessa arrived at Channel Five News TV studio for her interview with Priscilla Jones, only to be mobbed by a myriad of tabloid reporters. She hadn't counted on the journalistic grapevine to divulge her whereabouts so quickly. As they crowded around her car, she spotted the weekly tell-all mag reporters that had tried to get an insight into her private life and failed. That hadn't stopped them inventing stories to fill their gossip columns. She also saw writers from the Architecture Journal and LonProp, both prominent publishers of the latest news in London's property markets.

'Unbelievable,' she said at the sight. *How can the closure of the centre be so bloody important?*

She couldn't believe the attention Heidi Cross had garnered with her one humble clip on the local news. Taking care not to hit any of the vultures shouting out questions, she drove her car into the VIP car park and lost them in her rear-view mirror.

'Scandal, Ms O'Neil?' the parking manager joked with her as she hurried for the lift.

'Soon will be, if they can help it. It's ludicrous, isn't it?' she said, wondering if he secretly agreed with Heidi and her views.

'It certainly is. I'll make sure they stay away from the stairwells. Sneaky buggers, journalists.' He chuckled, but sounded sincere.

'Thank you,' Vanessa said quickly and stepped into the first vacant lift.

The maroon-carpeted cubicle was so peaceful. As the lift ascended she looked in the mirror, using the time to give herself a once-over. Having a well-known face and a prominent family name had its drawbacks. She always had to look her best, and even for her, it took a lot of work.

The face in the mirror was the same one that had been staring back at her for three decades, just a little fuller. It irked Craig—and even angered him unreasonably—that she had inherited her delicate features from their mother's side of the family, whilst he had inherited their father's thickset genes.

Perhaps his resentment for her was also down to the fact that a few of his girlfriends ended up falling for her when he brought them home; this happened so often that he stopped inviting her to his 'love me I'm rich' booze-fuelled parties. Unlike Craig, Vanessa stayed away from too much alcohol. She'd made martial arts about more than just defence training, turning it into a weekly fitness regime that kept her fit and healthy.

Just as the doors clicked open, Vanessa tucked in the last ear of shirt that had come loose from her belt as she'd raced from her car; away from the cameras still trying to catch a shot of her. She shook her head as she remembered being listed as one of London's Rebel Rich.

'Young up-and-coming women who live life by their own rules' was the tag line in the article, which had run in the business section of The London Times the year before. *Well, rebel rich girl, time to use your charm.*

Vanessa trotted along the carpeted corridor. She loathed being late for anything, even for something as mundane as a dentist appointment, let alone a television interview.

'Ms. O'Neil,' Priscilla called from her left as she scanned the room for the tall blonde woman with the sexy voice. 'Over here.'

After brief introductions and a quick chat, Vanessa sat hooked up to a microphone under glaring lights, ready to be interviewed. Priscilla gave her a reassuring wink, obviously under the impression that Vanessa was nervous. The very thought made Vanessa want to laugh. She dealt with much more intimidating situations in the boardroom on a daily basis; this interview was going to be a walk in the park in comparison.

If she did seem off balance, it was because Heidi Cross' appearance had taken her by complete surprise. To make matters worse, she had insulted her too. Yes, Heidi was as gorgeous as she looked on TV but that's where the attraction ended. *To think I thought she was compassionate. Judgemental more like. Saying I was worse than Craig—the cheek of it.*

'Are you ready?'

Vanessa gave Priscilla her best smile and pushed all thoughts of her encounter with Heidi out of her mind. This was business. She needed to be focused. 'Yes. Whenever you are.'

'Okay. So, tell me, Ms. O'Neil—'

'Please, call me Vanessa,' she offered amicably.

'Uh, yes. Right. Why the Young Mind's building?' Priscilla asked, clutching a piece of paper covered in illegible writing.

'Why that building in particular?' Vanessa repeated her question because she needed time to formulate an answer that the viewers would accept. In all honesty, it was just down to money. Craig had been ecstatic at the price he had knocked the owner down to.

'The owner regrettably passed away and left the building to his son, who approached us for a possible sale. After inspection, we found the location of the site ideal which, to an astute business owner, is key to sound investment.'

Priscilla's static smile and strategically crossed knees remained frozen in time for the camera. 'And what will Berkley O'Neil do with the building?' Priscilla asked politely. 'I mean, why demolish an entire building when you have four others with better potential?'

'What we at Berkley O'Neil strive to do with these developments is create jobs and prosperity for the local communities of the properties we procure,' Vanessa replied smoothly. Her mind wandered back to Heidi. Vanessa hoped she was watching this interview, so she could see how wrong she was about her. *I am not like Craig.*

'And in doing so, you intend to take away the valuable service that Young Minds is providing for young people in need,' Priscilla retorted instantly. The bite in her tone felt almost personal.

'That is not what we are doing ....' Vanessa needed

to concentrate. Thoughts of Heidi had free reign in her brain and were distracting her. 'Sorry, can you repeat the question?'

'I said by closing down the centre you're taking away a service for vulnerable young people.'

'Admittedly, it's difficult for people not in our line of business to understand how we operate, so let me explain it for you and the viewers.'

It was time to do some spinning. Get the viewers on her side. 'There are people who need to find jobs, qualified people, who worked hard for their accreditations and are now left unemployed because unproductive institutions are occupying buildings like these. How is that fair to hardworking students and professionals?'

'But do you ever consider those who lose their livelihoods through your acquisitions?' Priscilla persisted.

Vanessa smiled as she steered the conversation away from what she knew was a sensitive subject. Priscilla was using 'acquisition' as a synonym for 'ripping off the poor'. Heidi had done the same with her corporations-are-heartless-bastards speech.

'Once the building has been demolished, we will establish exciting new businesses like restaurants and coffee bars to make this part of London thrive even more,' she said, trying not to sound like a game show host. 'This amazing transformation will be complete within the next two years, vastly improving the status of Kentish Town and helping local businesses attract a more high-end clientele.'

'Progress, then,' Priscilla reiterated.

'That's correct,' Vanessa said. 'Berkley O'Neil sees the potential Kentish Town offers and the new life it can attract once the neighbourhood is put to better use.'

'Like ultimately pushing up property prices as well as rental rates?' Priscilla came at her from nowhere.

The amicable woman who was sitting there only five minutes before was gone, replaced by a cobra slowly constricting her body before finally going in for the kill.

'Eventually, all the working-class people and students who now call Kentish Town home will have to leave their beloved neighbourhood because they'll have been pushed out,' Priscilla said. 'The very people who make Kentish Town what it is—a cosmopolitan area—wouldn't be able to afford to live there anymore.'

'I disagree,' Vanessa pushed back. 'As with all new builds in this area, a proportion of the apartments we build will be affordable homes.'

'I think our ideas of "affordable homes" are probably worlds apart, Vanessa,' Priscilla said with her frozen smile and a cheerful tone. 'So, tell us what you think of leaving the hardworking people at the Young Minds Centre unemployed? Is your company aware of the good work they do there?' she continued. 'We recently spoke to their manager, Heidi Cross, who issued a public plea for the charity's survival. Do share with us your thoughts on the situation. And how, as a prominent lesbian, evicting a gay charity doesn't seem like a stab in the back to those in your own community.'

Why the hell does my sexuality have to define who I am?

But Vanessa knew she had to say something that would appease her, as Priscilla clearly wasn't going to let it drop.

'Priscilla, believe me the last thing I would do is stab anyone in the back. As it happens I share Heidi's concern about what the future holds for the charity.' She smiled without parting her lips. 'And that's why I've postponed all of my engagements for tomorrow to pay them a visit to see how I can help,' she added quickly.

Of course she hadn't really, but she was losing ground and needed a quick get out clause. Now Vanessa would have to grant Heidi Cross a face-to-face meeting. *I hope she's satisfied. This is the first and last thing that woman will ever get from me.*

Chapter Six

Lying bitch.

Kelli switched off the TV and threw the remote control down on her bed. She'd just watched the news segment about the closure of Young Minds and the uproar from the community. Some opposed it but others wanted the closure if it meant bringing jobs into the neighbourhood. Kelli pitied the idiots. The tactics Berkley O'Neil used were typical: send in the 'hot woman' to win the public over then, while no one's looking, do whatever the hell they want. She'd seen this game played out so many times and it sickened her. Kelli couldn't believe that anyone with more than one brain cell could be taken in by the claptrap these news outlets were spewing. *And people say teenagers are thick.*

Kelli was considering what to do with herself for the rest of the day, when she heard a knock on her bedroom door. She wasn't expecting anyone. It was way too early in the day for it to be Vanessa. Knowing her, it would be midnight before she finally managed to drag herself away from the office. *Not that I give a damn.*

Before Kelli could ask who was there, the door pushed open and Jason stood in the doorway. Thick, dark hair framed his round face.

'Hi, Kelli,' he said quietly.

'Jason,' she said, gesturing for him to come in. She wasn't rude about his unexpected intrusion but she wasn't exactly welcoming either.

Unfazed, he strode into her room, which thankfully she had tidied that morning. Normally she left things until it was a battle to enter or exit, but that suited her fine; it kept Vanessa at bay.

Kelli flopped down on the bed and looked up at him. 'What's up?'

'Nothing much,' he said, lowering himself onto the edge of her bed.

They were both silent for a few moments before Jason spoke again. 'I came round to see if you'd told your aunt you've been suspended from college.'

Kellie frowned. Jason knew how she felt about sharing things with Vanessa, so she knew straight out he was lying. Adults weren't the only ones guilty of it.

She ignored the question and took out a can of beer from her stash under the bed. 'Do you want one?'

Jason shook his head and averted his gaze. For a guy as good-looking as Jason, he didn't have much confidence, whereas scrawny, spotty teenagers walked around like they were God's gift to women.

'Did you mean what you said in your text? About, you know ….'

Yes, she knew. The text she'd finally sent in reply to him about Evan. Kelli cracked open a beer and drank deeply. The can was half empty by the time she looked at Jason to address his question.

'Of course I didn't sleep with him. I wouldn't have sex with Evan if he was the last boy on earth,' she said, with meaning in her voice because it was true.

Jason glanced over at her and a slight smirk touched his lips.

Booze-fuelled, Kelli was going to tell him she wouldn't date him either but managed to stop herself in time. *Why should I hurt him just because I'm hurting?*

Instead, she jerked up into a sitting position and said, 'Wanna play Xbox?'

Jason didn't look like he was leaving any time soon and Kelli wasn't in the mood for talking, so if he stayed he'd have to be content with her playing her game.

'Okay,' he said, slipping out of his jumper. As he lifted his top he exposed his well-toned stomach. He gave her a knowing look and Kelli's eyes widened and her eyebrows rose. *If he only knew.*

Kelli turned away but not before she saw the disappointment in his eyes.

She drained the rest of her beer and threw it under the bed, making a mental note to put it in the bin before she went to sleep. The last thing she needed, on top of everything else, was for her aunt to have a go at her about her drinking habits.

Kelli pushed herself to her feet then went over to the glass TV unit and switched on the game. Two hours later, with hundreds of zombies killed and just enough points to move to a level she'd never reached before, she felt a tap on her shoulder. Spooked, Kelli jerked forward. She'd been so wrapped up in her game that she'd almost forgotten Jason was there.

'I'm gonna make a move,' he said, standing.

'All right,' she mumbled as she turned back to the

screen.

'Aren't you going to walk me to the door?' he asked.

'Oh shit!' she cried out as a zombie rounded on her character and bit greedily at its neck. Lack of concentration had got her killed.

'All right, let's go,' she said, hiding the irritability from her voice. Kelli wouldn't mind acting the perfect host if she'd invited him round, but she hadn't.

Kelli trailed behind Jason as they made their way downstairs. Once outside, they stood awkwardly on the doorstep. Jason shifted from foot to foot and looked at everything but Kelli.

A slight wrinkle formed between his eyebrows and a minute later, he asked, 'Don't you like me, Kelli?'

Kelli stalled. She wanted to tell him the truth but the words caught in her throat. At that moment, she realised she was just like all the adults in her life after all.

Jason closed his eyes for a brief moment as if steeling himself for her response. The last thing Kelli wanted to do was hurt him. She actually liked him, just not in the way he wanted. If only things had been different. Her stomach twisted as she leant against the doorframe and crossed her legs at the ankle.

'You're a great guy, Jason. I'd just prefer to take things slow,' she lied. She leant forward, and kissed his cheek then retreated indoors … before she was forced to lie again.

Chapter Seven

'Go on try it.'

'Try what, Natalie?' Vanessa asked.

'Say Heidi Cross without that faraway look in your eyes.'

'A faraway … What? You're kidding me right?'

'Nope, she rattled you in a good way. I can tell.' Natalie swept her long dark dreadlocks over her shoulder in one swift movement. 'Go on. Admit it.'

Sitting in Raffles Wine Bar at a table overlooking the bustling streets of Soho, Vanessa was now reminded why she shouldn't have mentioned her earlier encounter with Heidi to Natalie. If she'd known Natalie would read more into it than there was, she would have kept her thoughts to herself.

'I'm beginning to wish I'd have come out alone with Kay tonight,' Vanessa said gesturing to Natalie's sister, whose back was turned to them.

Although Natalie and Kay were twins; they were polar opposites. Natalie was gay, Kay was straight and married with two kids. Natalie dressed immaculately in designer clothes, Kay felt more at home in jeans and a football shirt. Natalie was organised in every area of her life to a point of obsession while Kay took each day as it came, much to Natalie's annoyance. Yet, despite their differences, the bond between them was undeniably strong.

'Oh my God, that was a bloody foul!' Kay's gaze was locked on the football match showing on a large flat screen TV. The whole bar was enthralled as Arsenal battled it out with Bournemouth. It was 2-1 to Bournemouth with only minutes to go until the final whistle. 'Come on ref, what the hell are you doing?'

Vanessa had not planned to spend her evening with one twin engrossed in football and the other trying to bulldoze her into admitting to feeling something she didn't. They were meant to be catching up as they hadn't seen each other for the past two weeks. Vanessa wanted to hear about Natalie's boathouse renovation project and how Kay's training for a marathon was going. So far she knew nothing of either.

'So, come on, out with it.'

Vanessa knew Natalie wouldn't let the subject of Heidi Cross drop until she admitted to something, anything, even if it wasn't true. A good, loyal friend for the past fourteen years, Natalie thought she knew Vanessa inside out. On most things she did, Vanessa admitted, but this time she couldn't have been further from the truth.

Staring at Vanessa with amused hazel eyes, Natalie waited to hear her admit that she found Heidi undeniably attractive. For a split second, an image of Heidi swam into Vanessa's mind and she inwardly shuddered at seeing the anger that distorted her features. Attractive Heidi might well be, but her attitude left a lot to be desired. Even hearing her name made Vanessa squirm, a far cry from how she'd felt when she had first seen her on TV.

'I have nothing to—'

Kay suddenly leapt to her feet, cradling her head in her hands. 'That was a fucking dive! Jesus Christ, I give up! The ref is obviously getting a backhander.'

As the final whistle blew, a loud roar of elation erupted in the bar for the winning team. Kay slumped into her chair and picked up her bottle of water. 'I'm so done with football. It's pathetic.'

'Hmm, how many times have we heard that one?' Natalie said with a wry smile.

'It's true. I'm going to end up having a heart attack at this rate.' Kay took a mouthful of water. 'So what've you two been bitching about while my stress levels were rising?'

'Do you really need to ask?' Vanessa said.

Natalie wiggled her eyebrows. 'Women, of course.'

'And there's me thinking I'd missed out on stimulating conversation,' Kay said. 'Natalie, why don't you do the world a favour and give up on women. Relationships obviously aren't for you.'

'You say that like it's my fault that I can't be dealing with women and their drama,' Natalie said.

'But you'd be more than happy for me to be involved with someone who compared me to my brother?' Vanessa cut in. 'No, sorry, who thinks I'm worse than him.'

'I'm sure it wasn't personal,' Natalie said. 'You have to think of her like a lion protecting her cub.'

'And how would you know what her motive is?

You saw her on TV for, what, a minute?' Vanessa asked incredulously.

'That was long enough to suss her out. But then again, what do I know? Look at the mistake I made with Angela.' Natalie briefly cast her eyes downwards.

'You guys broke up again?' Vanessa said.

'Yep. She finally tipped me over the edge.'

'Why?'

''Cause she's had enough of being sea sick?' Kay said with an air of distaste.

'There's nothing wrong with living on a boat, thank you. Anyway, we broke up because Angela's frigging mood swings are off the scale.' Natalie's manicured nails tapped gently on the side of her glass. 'Seriously, if I bought her chocolates, she'd get in a mood because "I'm on a diet" or "What are you trying to do, make me fat?" If I bought them for myself and didn't offer her one, she'd go mental calling me "selfish". God help me if I reminded her that she was on a diet, I'd get the third degree. "What do you mean. Do you think I need to diet? So you're admitting I'm fat?" I mean, how the hell do you cope with a woman like that?'

'Replace the chocolates with flowers?' Vanessa suggested, 'You can still take her on a romantic break to Paris to make up.'

Natalie rolled her eyes. 'In which sentence did you hear me say I wanted her back?'

Vanessa laughed. 'Oops, sorry.'

'What I need is to meet someone hormonally

balanced. So if you're not interested in that Heidi woman, tell her your best friend—'

'Who wants the impossible,' Kay interjected with a smirk.

'Is single and ready to mingle,' Natalie said ignoring Kay's comment.

'I'm sure she'll go weak at the knees when she hears that,' Kay mocked.

'I've told you, I'm going to see her to save face, nothing else,' Vanessa said. 'And I certainly don't want her being involved with you.'

'Why not?'

'Because she's offensive, hot headed—'

'And ridiculously gorgeous,' Natalie said with a grin.

'Even if she is, that doesn't excuse her blatant rudeness.'

'Get real, Nessie, she'd never be able to top Craig on that score.'

'And you think that makes it all right?'

'No, but have you thought the whole name-calling episode could have been avoided if you had treated her a little better?' Natalie asked cautiously.

'What?! Are you saying it's my fault she turned on me?'

'No, of course not,' Natalie said quickly. 'But it wouldn't have killed you to hear her out for a few minutes.'

'I didn't have a few minutes. I was on my way to the studio to be interviewed. You know I don't like being late for appointments.'

'Listen to you two going round in circles,' Kay said sighing. 'I can wrap this up for you right now, Vanessa. When you see her tomorrow, give her your prettiest smile and apologise for being an arsehole.'

Vanessa opened her mouth but Kay shot her a warning look.

'Yes, Vanessa, you were an arsehole. Just own it.'

'Yeah, and you never know where tomorrow might lead,' Natalie added. 'For all you know, fate could have set you both on a collision course. You were meant to meet.'

If that was the case, Vanessa would rather have met Heidi at a bar. Not under these circumstances, where Heidi's only intention was to bring down her family's company.

***

The balmy evening had turned into a frigid night, Vanessa realised as she drove slowly through the quiet streets of London with the heating on full blast. She was thankful her day was nearly over, it couldn't have gone any worse. First, Heidi had ambushed her in the lobby of her office, then she had found herself staring down a double-barrelled shotgun while being interviewed on TV, forcing her to publicly state her intention to visit the centre. And the final nail in the coffin had been Natalie and Kay defending Heidi's actions. After giving their words some thought, Vanessa decided she wasn't in the wrong. You couldn't just go around confronting people because you didn't like a decision they'd made. In her line of work, she always came across obstacles but that didn't mean she took a hammer to them, which seemed to be Heidi's way of dealing with things.

So what was the problem? Why did she still feel bad about their encounter despite her bravado in front of Natalie? Vanessa slipped into a reflective mood as she turned the car into her street. Large oak trees lined either side of the road, their branches swaying gracefully in the wind.

Vanessa had to admit her defences were heightened when Heidi had approached her out of the blue. Her sudden appearance had thrown Vanessa off balance. Her usually calm composure had crumbled at the sight of Heidi. The attraction had been intense, more so than when she first saw Heidi on TV. Meeting face-to-face didn't have the same security as the safety of her office.

She mentally cursed Craig for forcing her to step in and clean up his mess. He was the one responsible for the unexpected storm that was threatening to cause havoc in their lives. *When is he going to learn that he needs to choose his battles carefully.*

Vanessa steered her Aston Martin into the garage of her house in Kensington. Pushing aside thoughts of Craig and her impending meeting with Heidi the next day, she grabbed her laptop bag, climbed out of the car and made her way through the side door of the house. As Vanessa entered the hallway, she could hear Maggie banging pots and pans in the kitchen. At seventy-eight, Maggie still hadn't got her head around loading a dishwasher.

Maggie had been in Vanessa's life ever since she could remember. Her parents had employed her to look after Craig and herself when they were children and when they left home they kept her on as a housekeeper. Although she lived in her own small apartment a few houses away she had a key to Vanessa's house and came over most days to keep an eye on Kelli. As well as to check that Vanessa had eaten.

'Kelli?' Vanessa called out, in a bid to attract the attention of her niece. No reply.

'She's out,' Maggie's voice sounded before she came into view. She wore a black dress over her petite frame, and a black bow held back her shoulder length steel grey hair.

Oh great! More stress from worrying about Kelli's whereabouts. Vanessa could already feel a migraine coming on. Of course pushing the boundaries was to be expected from someone Kelli's age, but Vanessa was growing increasingly intolerant of her lack of communication. How much longer could they live in this bubble before it burst?

Kelli seemed to have undergone a personality change since her mother had died a year before. It suddenly occurred to Vanessa, barely a word was exchanged between them these days—unless Kelli wanted something that is. As much as Vanessa would have liked to have thrown in the towel, she accepted that it was her responsibility to ensure Kelli survived her mother's death and the terrible pain and guilt she'd left in her wake. Vanessa was ashamed to admit she was doing a lousy job of it by the looks of things. It didn't help that Kelli looked so much like her mother; she had the same shoulder length blonde hair and dark lashed blue-grey eyes, that sometimes it was too painful to even look at her. Vanessa didn't care to remember how many times she'd come close to calling her Lauren.

'She'll be back soon,' Maggie said. 'If you're like this now, what are you going to do when she turns eighteen? She'll be a law unto herself.'

'I know,' Vanessa admitted. 'But ....'

Maggie gave her a sympathetic look. 'I know. I know. You can't help but worry. That's exactly what your mother used to say about you when you went out with your friends.'

Vanessa sighed. 'I need a drink.'

Maggie folded her arms over her chest and stared Vanessa down like a reprimanding mother. 'And what's that going to achieve?'

'Oblivion, if I drink enough,' Vanessa said, heading to her home office.

'And when you wake up tomorrow the problem will still be there.'

Vanessa knew Maggie was right but she didn't care. She needed something to take the edge off. She switched the light on, walked over to the drinks cabinet and poured a measure of brandy.

Maggie stood in the doorway and shot her a disapproving look.

'Okay, okay, I'll only have a few.'

Maggie cocked her head.

Vanessa laughed. 'Okay, a couple. Deal?'

Maggie remained silent. Instead her gaze dropped to the opened letter lying on Vanessa's desk.

Maggie's brown eyes studied Vanessa's face until she felt compelled to speak, if only to spare them both the awkwardness of silence.

'I know I should have brought the suspension up with Kelli, but now isn't the right time. I'm scared to push her any further.' Vanessa paused. She was tired of hiding behind a mask of happiness. Pretending everything was okay. Because it wasn't. Far from it. And if there was one person she could come clean with, it was Maggie. Confidant and friend of her parents, Vanessa could tell Maggie how she felt and not expect a sermon or judgment.

She raked her fingers through her hair. It was as if her thoughts were desperate for release, regardless of whether she actually wanted to say them out loud. Like water, they poured from her lips before she could stop them.

'I feel like I'm letting her down because of my own weaknesses and inability to work through this mess,' Vanessa said, clutching her glass like a buoy in a stormy sea. 'Maggie, tell me straight: am I letting Kelli down the way I did Lauren?'

Maggie was by her side in seconds. Her liver-spotted hand stroked Vanessa's hair away from her face, just like it did when she was a child, waking up from a bad dream.

'Don't let me hear you talking like that young lady. Ever. You did not let your sister down. For whatever reason, Lauren made her own decision and it had nothing, and I mean nothing to do with you.'

'But I—'

'Vanessa, listen to me. There's nothing you can do for Lauren now. She's gone. But Kelli … she's still here. She knows you'll always be there for her, so give her the space to withdraw and deal with her pain in her own way. She'll come out of herself soon enough, and when she does, she's going to need you more than ever to help her face a life she doesn't want to face. Until then, just be a dry leaf on the river bank for her.'

'Go with the flow, you mean?' Vanessa asked, her voice breaking while she swallowed down the lump in her throat.

'Yes, go with the flow.'

If only it was that easy.

'Right.' Maggie snapped back into her usual control mode. 'I'd better get back to cleaning the kitchen. I don't know how it gets into such a terrible state.'

Vanessa smiled through her tears. 'I don't know what I'd do without you, Maggie.'

'Well it's a good thing I'm not going anywhere,' Maggie said, gently patting Vanessa's cheek. 'Now, have another drink if you must but I don't want to see you falling up the stairs like some scatty teenager. I had enough of that when you were eighteen.'

Maggie grinned at Vanessa then left the room.

Although Maggie's advice seemed bleak, waiting

for Kellie to come round was going to be her only
option. The fact that Kelli wasn't ready to talk to her
about Lauren's death was understandable. Vanessa
could barely make sense of the tragedy herself. The pain
came from not knowing what had tipped Lauren over
the edge and made her think the only way out was to
take her own life. That she couldn't, wouldn't confide
in Vanessa about her troubles. If she had, Vanessa
would have moved heaven and earth to help her. Laid
down her own life for her without a second thought.
But deep down, she knew it was more complicated than
that. To do something so drastic, so final, Lauren must
have been at her wit's end. What other explanation
could there be for a mother to leave her child behind?
A daughter who she loved more than anything.

All that was left now was a nightmarish mystery
that was so raw, none of her family could touch it. In
typical O'Neil fashion, they left the giant elephant in the
room and walked around it every day instead. Her grief
was like an ironclad demon with a firm grip on her heart.
It still enveloped her every step and breath she took.
Lauren hadn't just ended her life, she had also ended the
secure, happy life Vanessa once took for granted.

She glanced at the wooden, well-oiled grandfather
clock that stood in the corner. It was nearly midnight.
She was too awake to go to bed so she resorted to the
only thing that kept her mind occupied: work, her
saving grace.

Sitting at her desk, she pulled a pile of contracts
from the drawer. Losing herself in work was more

productive than thinking about Lauren's suicide and Kelli's downward spiral.

The first folder she opened held the contract for the Kentish Town building. *This is too much of a coincidence.* No matter how many times Vanessa tried not to think of Heidi Cross, she would come across something that reminded her of her. A comment on Twitter, a replay of Heidi's interview on TV, Natalie coming to Heidi's defence and now the contract for the centre she managed.

'Heidi Cross,' she whispered to the background music of pattering rain, her name sounded as sweet as she was beautiful. 'Why have you come into my life?'

Thankfully, she wouldn't have to wait much longer to find out the answer.

Chapter Eight

Heidi thanked the stars, the sun, and the moon for giving her another chance to set things straight with Vanessa. It was only yesterday that she had all but given up on the centre. That was until Vanessa's TV interview was aired. She could have got down on her knees and kissed Priscilla Jones' feet for railroading Vanessa into being accountable for the decisions her family business made.

Heidi had barely slept during the night because of this. It was agonising waiting to see if Vanessa would keep her word. To her credit, Vanessa's secretary had called minutes earlier to announce that Vanessa would drop by later that morning.

Heidi's plan of action was to start off on the right foot this time and apologise for her unprofessional behaviour. To try and make Vanessa understand that despite her first impressions, she wasn't normally rude and abrupt. Rather that she was quite amicable once you got to know her. The sooner they moved on from the incident at Vanessa's offices, the sooner they could focus their attention on what really mattered. The centre.

'I'm glad you're all here,' Heidi said as she walked into the conference room, taking a moment to sip her coffee. She stopped at the head of the table. 'Contrary to what I said yesterday, it seems publicising the eviction had the desired effect.'

All eyes focused on her. Hoping, praying that somehow a miracle had taken place.

'Vanessa O'Neil is coming here to speak with me today.'

It took less than a second for the room to erupt with claps and hollers.

Heidi held up her hand to quieten them down. 'Hang on a minute. Now I don't want you to get your hopes up too much. Bear in mind this is most probably a publicity stunt to make the public think they're not the cold-hearted bastards I tried to portray them as.'

As she spoke, Simone entered the room and looked around. 'What have I missed?'

'Heidi has a date with Vanessa O'Neil,' Christina said with a wink.

Heidi coughed uncontrollably as she swallowed her coffee the wrong way at hearing Christina's comment.

'Hey are you okay?' Simone gently tapped her back.

Heidi nodded, as she inhaled and exhaled slowly. After a few seconds, she smiled at Simone who was eyeing her with concern. 'I'm fine, thanks.'

'I thought she only said that to shut the interviewer up,' Mel said when Heidi gestured for her to talk.

'So did I but her secretary just called,' Heidi said. 'I suppose she had to follow through.'

'Oh, I love Priscilla's tactics. Just when you think you're winning—bam—she has you on the ropes,' Christina said.

'And that's exactly what she did with Vanessa

yesterday,' Harry said.

'Good on Priscilla. I know she looks a bit clueless but that's what's so great about her. A wolf in sheep's clothing,' Simone said.

The others round the table nodded in agreement.

'So, we're only getting one crack at this and we have to hit the jackpot first time. This is not the lottery,' Heidi said seriously. 'We can't choose as many lines as we want. It's make or break.'

'What time is she coming?' Harry asked.

'At midday, which gives us …' Heidi glanced at her wrist watch, 'Exactly two hours to get this place into shape. I want all hands on deck. Anything that doesn't need to be on display I want gone—'

'We can hide all the junk in the store room. She won't need to look in there,' Kirsty piped up.

'Good idea,' Heidi said nodding. 'Right guys, let's get moving. And please make sure all hallways are mopped and swept. We want to give a good impression. I'll be in my office if anyone needs me.'

Time conscious, Heidi rushed back to her office. The place was a mess. Yes, she was happy that Vanessa was coming, *more like ecstatic*, but she really would have appreciated a little more than two hours' notice. It had taken many years for her office to get into the state it was in, so it was going to take a little longer than a couple of hours to clear it. Heidi rushed through her notes and gathered all the pertinent financial and social files. Sweat trickled down her back and her heart pumped more rapidly with every shift of the wall clock's arm.

Relief flooded her when Simone walked in an hour later. 'I thought you might need some help,' she said looking around the room. 'Looks like I was right. Your mother would be ashamed if she saw this place.'

'Ha ha, very funny. Instead of standing there, make those files disappear.'

Simone grabbed an armful of files stacked in a corner and, with all her weight, forced them into a dusty wall cabinet. 'If she doesn't change her mind after all this effort, I'll throttle her.' Simone groaned as she shoved the doors of the cupboard hard and slapped the padlock through the bolt before the folders could counterattack and tumble to the ground. Victorious, she clicked in the lock and grinned at her triumph.

Heidi applauded her and Simone gave a curtsy in return. 'Right, that's done, what else?'

'Open the windows. A quick wipe down of the desk and then ... we wait.'

Chapter Nine

Sunshine eluded Kensington even though the forecast didn't predict rain. From her kitchen window, Vanessa watched the shadows cast by clouds ebb and flow over the bushes in her garden. She was enjoying the tranquil atmosphere that crept over her like a soothing, cool stream when the moment was shattered by the sound of her mobile phone ringing.

Probably Gina, she told herself and answered the anonymous call.

'Ms O'Neil?'

Vanessa didn't catch the first part of the conversation. All she heard was, 'We have your niece in custody.'

'Jesus,' she muttered. It had taken one sentence for her day to fall to pieces.

Maggie walked into the kitchen holding a shopping bag and frowned, but her expression soon changed and Vanessa knew she'd guessed the call was about Kelli.

'I'm on my way,' Vanessa told the police officer. Her core temperature shot up to a near fever as she disconnected the call. 'Kelli just had to mess up my day, didn't she?'

Sorry, Heidi. Looks like we'll have to postpone destiny.

Maggie kept quiet while Vanessa punched in another number on her phone.

'Craig,' Vanessa said when he answered.

'What?' he growled. 'I'm right in the middle of a

meeting.'

'Of course you are. Just tell her to powder her nose for a minute while I talk to you,' she retorted. Being pissed off was strangely liberating.

'Just get to the point.'

'The police have Kelli. I have to go and pick her up.'

After a considerable silence with no insults or condescension, Craig said, 'Where exactly are you when she gets into trouble?'

'I don't have time for this. Just go to the centre and show your face,' she said. 'And for Christ's sake, look interested.'

She hung up before he could reply, knowing he wouldn't have anything constructive to say. Maggie simply shook her head sadly as Vanessa left to perform her duty as guardian for the girl she couldn't get through to.

Traffic was horrendous, as it always was when she had to get somewhere in a hurry.

When Vanessa finally arrived at the police station, a tired-looking desk officer was busy talking to someone on the phone. When she finished, she glanced up at Vanessa.

'Can I help you?' the police officer asked, adjusting her clothing and her hair.

'I'm here to pick up my niece, Kelli O'Neil.'

Vanessa made a point of not exploding in a torrent of shouts when Kelli strolled into the waiting area, guided by a tall, bald police officer with huge light blue eyes. He reminded her of an army sergeant, a man who took no crap from teenagers that's for sure.

'Ms. O'Neil, you're Kelli's aunt?' he said coarsely.

'Yes I am, officer,' she replied, slightly intimidated by the man's height.

'We picked her up at Highbury Station this morning, causing all manner of bother with a couple of lads,' he said, glancing at Kelli.

Kelli was dead quiet. She was obviously wary of the officer which was good—she needed someone to make her think about her actions. *Because I certainly can't.*

'I've told young Kelli here that she should be kept in for the day to teach her a lesson. I don't believe in rapping knuckles, Ms. O'Neil. I believe in stern reprimanding and a bit of discipline the first time round. You'd be amazed how few young repeat offenders we get if we teach them the ugly side of life.'

'I agree. I'll make sure that she's punished accordingly.'

Kelli didn't look at her. Instead she hung her head. Vanessa refused to enable her by asking what had happened, knowing that showing interest in delinquent conduct could be misconstrued as attention. She wouldn't give Kelli that at the risk of provoking similar outbursts.

'Good,' the officer said sternly. 'If I see her here again, there will be a more severe penalty.'

Kelli looked up at him as if to challenge his statement. The officer read Kelli's body language and pushed his chest out.

'Yes girl. Next time I'll misplace your aunt's number for a few hours while you're held over there,' he bellowed aggressively, pointing towards the holding cells down the hallway. 'In there you'll soon learn the true meaning of attention. We'll see how quickly you want to come back after a bit of a dance with our other guests. They don't have aunts to look out for them when they misbehave.'

The officer obviously didn't know Kelli's background, including her current emotional turmoil, but he was beginning to badger her and Vanessa felt Kelli had suffered enough.

'We should get going,' Vanessa said in a lighter tone.

She took hold of Kelli's arm with one hand and shook the officer's hand gratefully with the other before she marched Kelli out of the building.

'What the hell were you thinking?' Vanessa asked as she manoeuvred her car onto the dual carriageway and in the direction of home.

'Just leave me alone,' Kelli mumbled.

'Leave you alone? Do you really want that? Because if I do, you really will be on your own,' Vanessa snapped at her.

'Like you would know. You grew up with everything, right? Your life is so perfect with Mummy and Daddy's money.'

'You listen to me,' Vanessa retorted loudly, trying not to shout. 'Had it not been for my parent's money, you'd be way worse off than you are. And I'll tell you, kiddo, there's not much farther you can sink before you're buried.'

Kelli looked out of the window as they turned into their street.

'We haven't talked about your suspension yet. Don't think I didn't know,' Vanessa said, but Kelli simply ignored her.

Before she even parked the car, Kelli opened the door and jumped out.

'I'm talking to you!' Vanessa called out as she brought the car to a standstill.

'You're never home anyway "Aunty". What do you care?' she shouted back. 'I wish you were dead instead of my mother. At least she was there when I needed her.'

Kelli ran into the house.

Her words had sliced through Vanessa like a cleaver. She couldn't say much to that. Maybe Kelli was right. It should have been her. But it wasn't and unfortunately, Kelli was stuck with her—the incompetent aunt who had just as much trouble getting over Lauren's suicide as Kelli did. Vanessa hadn't been there when Lauren needed someone. The least she could do was to save her daughter from the same fate.

Chapter Ten

Kelli hadn't seen Vanessa so livid since the day of her mum's funeral, where she'd had heated words with Craig. *Maybe she's reached breaking point like I have.*

Kelli still couldn't believe the police officer had arrested her. She wasn't even being a nuisance. Two wannabe 'filmmakers' had thought she'd make for an entertaining 'punch and kick a stranger' YouTube video, but they'd got more than they'd bargained for when she retaliated. The martial arts lessons she used to take had paid off. Predictably, she was the one who got collared and accused of being disorderly for defending herself. *What a joke.*

Kelli tried to push the incident to the back of her mind by playing her Xbox, but it wasn't working. She couldn't forget the expression on Vanessa's face when Kelli told her she wished Vanessa had been the one that died.

Kelli regretted it the moment the words left her mouth, but it was too late to take it back. She'd only wanted Vanessa to feel her pain, which wasn't likely. Vanessa had no problem funnelling her attention into her work and pushing everything else to the side. It didn't make things easier to pretend her mum had never existed. Just because Vanessa didn't speak about her, it didn't mean Kelli would somehow forget her.

Kelli dropped the controller on the floor and rose

to her feet. For some time now she had wondered if it would be better if she left Vanessa's home. That way she wouldn't be a constant reminder of the unwanted responsibility Vanessa had been left.

Suddenly, a plan came to her. Kelli walked to her door and popped her head into the hallway. The TV was on downstairs which meant Maggie was occupied with Countdown. *Good. I can be in and out of Vanessa's office and she'll be none the wiser.*

Kelli was convinced Maggie only pretended to be busy around the house so she could spy on her and then give Vanessa a report of her movements for the day.

She crept along the hallway and entered Vanessa's office. The room smelt strongly of her perfume and for a minute, Kelli thought Vanessa might walk in behind her and give her a bollocking. She gave a quick glance over her shoulder but it was all clear. Good. *Now, where has she hidden my passport? I won't get far without it if I intend to leave this prison.*

Kelli searched in Vanessa's desk drawers. Nothing. She moved on to the filing cabinet, and was pleasantly surprised to find it open. She flicked through the tabs, startled to see one named 'Craig'. *Why is Vanessa keeping tabs on Craig?*

She withdrew the folder and pulled out the plans for the Kentish Town development, as well as sheets of financial papers. *What are they up to?*

Kelli slid onto the office chair and fanned the papers out in front of her, carefully scrutinising each of them. Some time later, she leant back and ran both her hands through her hair. *Oh boy, this just doesn't add up.*

Thoughts of what Kelli had originally been searching for were long forgotten. What she had just discovered was far more interesting.

Chapter Eleven

The preparations at the centre were finished just before midday. All members of staff stood proudly at the clean and tidy décor. Even Mel, who had an aversion to cleaning, had stayed right until the end, dusting and hoovering like it was going out of fashion. Heidi unscrewed a bottle of fizzy apple juice and poured everyone a glass. Lifting her plastic cup in the air she said, 'I'd like to propose a toast.'

They all followed suit.

'No matter how today turns out, I want you all to know that for five years, we've had great success in helping those who needed us.' The words caught in her throat. 'Regardless of what Vanessa and her company decide, we know that we did everything … we could.'

'To us!' Her colleagues' voices resounded as one.

'I'm late for my session with Lydia,' Richie said monotonously and made his way to his office down the hall.

'Beam of sunshine, that one,' Christina said before slurping her juice.

'She's here,' Simone called excitedly from where she was standing by the window. 'A car's just pulled up outside.'

A bolt of lightning shot through Heidi. The moment of truth had arrived. It was time to make amends.

Heidi descended the steps to reception as steadily as she could. In the entrance stood an overweight forty-something man. It wasn't until he took off his sunglasses that she recognised him. Craig O'Neil. Heidi looked towards the entrance waiting a few seconds for Vanessa to appear. Craig gave her a knowing look as she realised Vanessa wasn't coming. She had failed to keep her promise. *Why doesn't that surprise me?* Swallowing her disappointment, Heidi told herself she should be grateful that one of them had cared to show up.

Heidi plastered a smile on her face and held out her hand. 'Heidi Cross, manager of Young Minds.'

'If you say so, sweetheart.' Craig ignored her hand, brushed past her and started up the stairs.

'I thought your sister was coming today?' She ignored his slight and trailed behind him.

'Vanessa? Nah, she had better things to do,' he replied without taking the time to look at her. When he reached the landing, panting slightly, he said, 'Now, show me what's so great about this place.'

She persisted with her charm offensive and suppressed her rising anger. 'Can I get you something to drink before we start?'

'Whisky,' he said, checking out Simone's voluptuous form as she bent over to pick something up off the floor.

'I'm afraid we don't serve alcohol.' Heidi smiled to keep things relaxed. 'As you know we deal with teenagers—'

'Then I don't want anything. I'm not a teenager,

am I?' he scoffed, turning to her and ogling her cleavage without even trying to conceal it.

'No, you're not,' she said, feeling sick to her stomach. *You're an arsehole.* 'Come this way and I'll introduce you to our staff and explain what their roles are.'

Mentally counting to ten on loop, Heidi took Craig around the office, cheerfully introducing one colleague after the other. 'And we also run workshops every month for parents who need advice and support when they feel they're unable to connect with their children.'

Heidi gestured for Craig to follow her to the conference room, speaking as they walked.

'Gay and lesbian teenagers come to us for anything they might feel overwhelmed by. Most come to talk about how to find acceptance or about the hostility they may encounter from their families,' she recited in her most professional manner, wondering if anything was getting through to him.

'How about a session right now?' Craig asked as they entered the room.

'Our sessions are usually by appointment only,' she explained, ignoring his innuendo.

'No, sweetheart, you and me. Horizontal tango. Right here on this nice big table.' The corners of Craig's mouth curled upwards into a leery grin.

Heidi's hand itched to slap him, but she somehow managed to refrain. 'Not today, Mr. O'Neil.' She laughed, trying not to sound awkward. 'I have a schedule.'

He snorted at her reply. 'Do you offer sex workshops?'

'Sex therapy,' she corrected.

'You do? Hmm, I'm sure you're well qualified in that area,' he said grinning like an imp.

'Shall we move on?' Heidi said and quickly walked out of the empty room into the hallway. She could literally feel Craig's eyes undressing her and it sickened her.

'I tell you what, Heidi.' His words sounded like the prelude to a deal, maybe keeping her cool had actually paid off. 'Why don't we discuss the outcome of this building over dinner tonight? Maybe, if you play your cards right, we can work something out.'

There was no denying what he was suggesting and it was not what she wanted to hear.

'I'll tell you what, Craig. How about no?' It was at this point Heidi had had enough. She wouldn't normally allow anyone to talk to her the way Craig had, and she didn't care who he was or what carrot was dangling in front of her. She had more respect for herself. *What is it with these O'Neils?* 'I'm not that desperate and I really don't appreciate you wasting my time with your impotent attempts at flirting.'

'What did you say?' he sneered.

'I said: it's a good thing you're filthy rich because money is the only thing that could ever afford you sex.'

'Are you sure you want to insult me?' Craig asked, pressing his lips into a thin white line.

Heidi detected a quiver in his voice and saw

tremors in his hands. 'Oh, don't you like being rejected? That's odd, because I thought it was something you'd be used to by now.'

'How dare—'

'No, how dare you! You're paying us lip service and nothing more. You clearly don't give a damn about this organisation and you only showed up as a publicity stunt.'

'You have a loose mouth for someone who lives on the charity of others,' Craig retorted, raising his voice. 'Well, guess what? Your charity depends on rich men like me, sweetheart. I can have you on your knees begging just by flashing my wallet.'

'Not likely,' she said. 'Not even if my life depended on it.'

'I hope for your sake you have a cushy job lined up, because you and this place are done.'

'Get the hell out of here.'

Craig straightened and tugged down on his jacket with both hands. 'Don't you worry, I will.' A vein throbbed in his forehead and his face turned scarlet as he glared at her, eyes bulging. 'Fucking dyke. No wonder this place is struggling to stay in business. It's run by a bunch of fags and rug munchers who wouldn't know moral fibre if it strangled them.'

Heidi's body vibrated with rage. 'Get out, you homophobic prick!' she shouted after him as he ran down the stairs and stormed towards the entrance. He stopped abruptly in the doorway, gave her the finger and left.

If Heidi thought she felt awful before, it was a hundred times worse now.

Heidi brushed past her colleagues who had made their way into the hallway to see what the commotion was about, and raced to the ladies' toilet. She wanted to punch something, to scream, but all she could do was try and get her breathing under control. The mirror, as wide as the wall, was impossible to ignore and she was faced with the cause of Young Minds' unfortunate fate: her own reflection. She remained impassive staring sorrowfully at herself. She was so disappointed for losing it the way she had. No, it was worse than that. She was horrified. All she wanted was to rewind the last twenty minutes and start all over again. For the exchange to never have happened. She stood there for several minutes and contemplated what to do next. The thought of falling into a massive black hole and disappearing was the most appealing idea. She couldn't remain holed up in the toilets forever. The coward in her wanted to sneak down the hallway and out of the building, but it wasn't in her nature to run away. She liked to face things head on. *And that's your problem.*

'Well go on then, big mouth,' she said to her reflection, noting that she looked like a deer caught in headlights. 'Time to face the music.'

Heidi was unbearably tense when she walked into the conference room. The dreary, grim atmosphere could be cut with a blunt knife. Her colleagues sat in an awkward silence. Faces sank as they all looked down in defeat. No one would meet her gaze.

It was obvious to everyone what she had done and, like her, they knew it was game over.

Chapter Twelve

After Vanessa dropped Kelli at the house, she went straight to the office. Selfishly, she needed a break from her. Once again, she wasn't home as Kelli kept reminding her, but she was at the end of her tether with Kelli's hostile behaviour. At least at work she could clear her mind of the hurtful words Kelli had hurled at her. *First Heidi Cross, now Kelli.* Vanessa was starting to feel like an emotional punch bag for anyone who didn't get their way.

She passed by Craig's office and was surprised the door was closed. *Something must be wrong. Craig never closes his door.* He liked watching what was going on in the reception area and listening to office chatter. He was an extrovert through and through, and couldn't take a piss without an entourage. Only two things could have caused a closed door today: a secretary on her knees under his desk or a catastrophic blow to his day. Either way, Vanessa wanted to get an update about his visit to the centre.

She strode past his secretary and knocked on the door. 'Craig?'

'Come in if you have to,' he grunted in a muffled reply.

She opened the door and found Craig sat at his desk, shirt open to his sternum, drinking a large tumbler of dark liquid.

'Thirsty?' she asked.

'What's it got to do with you.' His words were less aggressive and more a sincere request for her to get off his back.

In no mood for the antics of a man-child, she got straight to the point. 'Did you go to the centre?'

Craig knocked back the last of his drink, grabbed the bottle and poured another.

'Easy,' she cautioned. 'You won't be able to get home at this rate.'

'What are you, my keeper?' he snapped, sitting back in his leather chair.

'Forget I said anything. Tell me what happened at the centre and I'll get out of your hair.'

Craig wiped his mouth with the back of his hand. 'I had the misfortune of meeting the slut that manages the place, that's what happened.'

Vanessa shook her head resenting being baited. 'Slut? Really?'

Craig looked unfazed. 'You have no idea what she's like. She practically sucked me off in the conference room.'

Does he actually think anyone believes the shit he makes up? 'But other than that, everything went okay?'

'I showed up didn't I?'

'That's the main thing.' Vanessa raised her eyebrows. 'I take it you still want to evict them?'

'You're damn right I do.' Craig pushed himself out of his seat and walked to the window. 'That woman has no business having any kind of influence over young, vulnerable minds.'

'Well, that's not our problem. I've got enough on my plate,' Vanessa said, retreating under Craig's judgemental gaze.

For the first time ever, Vanessa sat in her office and work wasn't on her agenda. Kelli was. An odd kind of detachment emerged as she relived their earlier clash. As if the hate and bitterness were directed at someone else—someone who deserved them. Kelli's harsh words led to so many questions, each of them begging an answer. But answers were something Vanessa didn't have access to. She only had the mental torment from each demon that gnawed at her.

Why does Kelli hate me? Why didn't Lauren call me that night? What made Lauren leave Kelli behind? More importantly, where was I when my sister needed me?

Vanessa reflected. *It seems I'm never there for anyone.* Not really. Not family and definitely not for the women she'd had casual, meaningless sex with. She could barely remember their faces. Each encounter had left her with a dark void until it reached a point where she gave up trying to connect with anyone. It was quite telling that Vanessa couldn't even own a pet; that's how messed up she was about commitment. *And yet Lauren thought I'd be able to look after Kelli.*

Her thoughts drove her deeper into a guilt-induced spiral. Suddenly Vanessa thought back to when she'd last seen Heidi. A vision of her face flashed up in Vanessa's mind. The pleading in her eyes as she tried to reach out to her, asking for help. *And what did I do?*

Turned my back on her. How much courage did it take for her to come and see me?

She needed to apologise. To hear her voice. Without further thought Vanessa dialled the number for the centre. When Heidi answered she almost stuttered but managed to keep her voice level. 'Heidi?'

'Who's this?'

'Vanessa … O'Neil.'

'What do you want?'

'To talk.'

'About?'

Silence. *What do I want to talk about? Seeing her again? What can I offer her?* 'The other day when—'

'Is this some kind of sick game you and your brother play? Trying to see who can be the most insufferable?'

'Heidi.' Just saying her name made Vanessa feel flustered. 'If Craig—'

'I'd rather not think about him—or you for that matter.'

I knew that bastard had been up to no good. Vanessa should have known better than to send Craig to the centre. She picked up a pen and scribbled absent-mindedly on a note pad. *I don't even want to think about what he must have done to upset her.*

Sensing Heidi's intention to hang up Vanessa said quickly, 'What do you want me to say?'

'How about you apologise for not showing today and for sending that brute of a brother instead—'

'I know what you must think—'

'What? That your parents must be disappointed having both an insensitive daughter and a horrible son?'

'No, that you think I intentionally bailed on you today.'

'Are you saying you didn't?'

'I had a family emergency. If I say I'm going to do something I do it.'

'Just not in this case.' Heidi blew out a controlled breath. 'Look, it's been a long day—'

'I get that my brother's visit wasn't a pleasant one—'

'That's an understatement.'

Vanessa gripped her phone tighter. 'And I feel really bad about it.'

'Not as bad as me.'

'I want to make amends.' *Where am I going with this?* Vanessa didn't like to feel unsure about anything—until now. Being in uncharted waters with Heidi felt almost liberating.

Vanessa remembered the way Heidi's gaze had flickered between her mouth and eyes, almost as if she couldn't decide whether she wanted to kiss Vanessa or simply lose herself in her gaze. *At least she did before she lost it.* An unstoppable force of desire invaded Vanessa's body. A tidal wave of excitement spread slowly throughout at the thought of … *Don't do it, don't think of her like that,* a voice in the back of her mind screamed for attention, but it was too late. Vanessa's mouth opened and the words flowed out. 'I'll drop by in the morning.'

'Is there any point?'

A soft inhale. 'I don't know, Heidi. That's up to you to decide.'

Chapter Thirteen

Kelli stood across the road from the Young Minds Centre, pretending to be talking on her mobile phone, but discreetly watching several people around her age enter and leave the building. She almost panicked when a woman with red hair appeared at the window on the first floor. Kelli doubted she could see her, but she couldn't be too careful. It was then that the familiar roar of Vanessa's car became audible. She was on time for her meeting with the manager of the centre. Kelli had overheard her talking on the phone to her secretary earlier and she'd felt compelled to come along and watch from a distance.

Ignoring the rain that had started to fall, she quickly ducked for cover behind the trunk of a thick oak tree, conveniently situated at the edge of the pavement. She pressed her body flat against the rough bark and didn't dare move for fear of drawing attention to herself. From her vantage point, she could see Vanessa's every move.

Vanessa's car came to a halt down an alleyway at the side of the building. Through the back window, Kelli could see her fixing her make-up in the rear-view mirror before exiting her car. Her shoulder-length hair was immaculate, as were her clothes. If there was one thing Kelli wanted that Vanessa had, it was her confidence. The woman had bucket loads of it. You could tell by the way she walked with her head held high and her back straight as a rod.

Within a minute, she had disappeared through the open door of the building. Kelli kicked the ground. *Now what do I do?* She didn't even know why she was there. *Yes, you do. Admit it.* Her skin crawled as if an army of ants were marching through her veins. 'Never,' she mumbled underneath her breath. She felt like an impatient horse, frustrated at being held up in the stalls before a big race.

Rubbing the back of her neck, she paced the pavement. *Is there any point hanging around?*

Knowing Vanessa, she'd be in there for ages, trying to give off the impression she was one of the good guys and there to help.

That was one of the many things that annoyed Kelli about Vanessa. She had all the time in the world when it came to business, but Kelli was always last in line. It angered her to know Vanessa cared more about her precious car than her own niece.

Kelli walked past the alley where Vanessa's car was parked, its black hood gleaming in the sun. She halted and retraced her steps. *I'll show her.* She strode down the alleyway, glancing over her shoulder to make sure no one was watching. When she was sure the coast was clear, Kelli took a penknife from her rucksack, moved to the front of the car and knelt down. In one swift movement, she stabbed at the tyre but the rubber was too tough to penetrate. Kelli kept stabbing it again and again with the force of hatred guiding her. A perverse sense of satisfaction hit her when the air spluttered from the tyre and it slowly flattened to the ground. Inching her way around to the other three tyres, she slashed and stabbed until she was spent. A slow smile crept across her lips as she pictured Vanessa's face when she saw the damage done to her precious car.

It's a shame my pain isn't as visible.

Kelli stood and walked back towards the street, her head tucked against her chest. The black hoody and jeans she wore were nondescript, so even if someone saw her leaving the area there was little chance of them describing her face. That was until she found herself shoulder-to-shoulder with another body. The collision knocked her sideways. She was now facing the woman who she'd bumped into.

'Hey, be careful,' the woman said.

Instinctively, Kelli looked up into the face of a woman who seemed a couple of years older than her. She had dark curly hair and blue eyes so deep you could drown in them.

'Sorry,' Kelli mumbled.

The woman wiped the rain from her forehead with the back of her hand. 'What's the matter? Scared of a bit of rain?'

She reached over and took Kelli's forearm loosely in her hand. Kelli shrugged it off roughly. She was a bundle of nerves and her muscles were twitchy. Vanessa could appear at any second or see her through a window of the centre. The last thing she needed was this stranger holding her up.

'What the fuck? Don't touch me.'

The woman laughed and jerked her head towards the building. 'Easy. I volunteer at the centre.'

'And?' Kelli's face flushed hot.

She works at the centre. Does that mean she's …?

'And … I saw you hiding behind the tree.' Her body language was open and easy.

'Well if you saw me, I couldn't have been hiding, could I?' The raw aggressiveness in Kelli's voice rang in her ears.

'In that case, you must be one of those new-age tree-huggers,' she said suppressing a grin. 'With you pressing up against it so hard, it was difficult to tell what you were doing.'

Kelli took a threatening step towards her and the woman shuffled backwards, holding her hands up in mock surrender. 'I'm kidding. You know, joking? You do know what a joke is, right?'

Kelli pulled a face. 'Do I look like I'm laughing?'

'No. You look troubled. It's a look I recognise.' The woman gave her a sympathetic smile that made Kelli's eyes sting. 'Look, if you ever want to talk, come and see me. My name's Christina.'

Christina stretched out her hand. Kelli looked down and ignored it. She carried on despite Kelli's slight. 'You can ask for me at reception and we can go for a coffee or a walk if you prefer.'

Kelli's mouth was dry and her heartbeat pounded against her ribcage. 'What the hell makes you think I have anything to say to you?'

Christina shrugged. 'Maybe I'm wrong but if I'm right, the offer stands. I'm at the centre Monday to Wednesday.'

Christina turned and walked towards the building. Kelli wanted to call her back but the words wouldn't come out. Every nerve ending in her body buzzed as she broke into a trot and headed in the opposite direction.

Christina. She committed the name to memory—just in case.

Chapter Fourteen

Heidi couldn't ignore the rush of adrenaline pumping through her veins. She tried to convince herself it was to do with the pressure of saving the centre and not that Vanessa was due any minute.

'So after yesterday's catastrophe, you're actually inviting another O'Neil to the office?' Simone sat on the edge of Heidi's desk, sipping a cup of tea.

'I wasn't about to turn her down. Not after the spectacle with her brother.'

The dark clouds finally opened and the rain arrived. It came down hard but Heidi liked it. Cool air drifted through the window and gently caressed her face.

'I wonder if she'll still come in this downpour,' Simone said, eyeing outside with disdain.

Heidi rose from her chair and walked over to the window. She gazed out in anticipation of Vanessa's arrival. Across the street, she could just about make out a figure standing behind the old oak tree and hoped, for their sake, no lightning struck.

Turning away from the window, Heidi glanced over at Simone. 'Don't you have work to do?' she teased. Although it was said in jest, Heidi urgently wanted her to leave so she could apply some make-up.

'I have a new client,' Simone said. 'But is there any point, since we don't know whether we'll even be around in a few weeks?'

'Of course there is. The music plays on until the very end,' Heidi said, the image of the stoic band members from *Titanic* popping into her mind.

'Okay, I'll leave you to prepare yourself for the arrival of Ms O'Neil. That's if she can be bothered to show up,' she said rolling her eyes.

Simone gently closed the door as she left Heidi's office which, after having been tidied the day before, was now almost back to its original mess.

After giving her cheeks a smudge of blusher and applying a faint layer of red, Heidi strolled towards the stairs that overlooked the entrance. Upon hearing the sound of rain pounding the pavement outside, Heidi absent-mindedly hummed *Singing in the Rain*. Imagining Gene Kelly tap-dancing, she soon followed suit with a few off kilter moves of her own.

'A woman of many talents I see.'

Shock winded Heidi. Her legs froze beneath her. She turned her head and came face-to-face with her real-life fantasy. She shivered as if a bucket of ice-cold water had been thrown over her. 'Vanessa!'

Vanessa smiled, making Heidi's heart flutter against her chest. The faded jeans she wore and the black shirt that outlined the contours of her body didn't help matters.

'I take it you're a fan of the film?'

Heidi wanted the floor to swallow her up in one big gulp. A dancer she was not. She knew it, and now Vanessa knew it too.

She waited for Vanessa to say something else. Maybe a comment on how awkward and stiff she moved or that her tapping had been out of sync, but instead she said, 'It's one of my favourites. There's nothing better than curling up in bed with the old classics.'

Heidi tried her hardest to refrain from imagining Vanessa in bed. *Remember she's the enemy here, not some knightess in shining armour.*

'So, did you find your way okay?' Heidi said eager to change the subject.

'Yes, and it's finally nice to meet you. Again,' Vanessa said extending her hand.

Heidi grasped it and was surprised when Vanessa held on a little longer than necessary.

Heidi was drawn to her like a magnet to metal. She wanted to freeze that moment. Just the two of them. Alone.

Standing feet apart in a narrow corridor, Heidi had the urge to grab her, to taste every part of her. Heidi's pulse hammered at the base of her throat as she stared at Vanessa's lips, and thought of all the places she'd like to feel them.

'Nice to meet you too. Look, about what I—'

'Forget about it—'

Stop staring at her breasts. 'But—'

'I deserved it. I had a lot on my mind that day.'

Heidi forced her eyes back up to Vanessa's face. 'I'm sorry anyway.'

'Me too.'

Something unspoken in Vanessa's gaze caused Heidi's knees to weaken. Controlling her nerves was impossible, no matter how hard she tried. What Heidi wouldn't have given to know what Vanessa was thinking. A flush rose to her cheeks as she wondered if they were as X-rated as her own thoughts.

Heidi waited for Vanessa to speak again, to break the spell, but she didn't. Which left it up to Heidi. *But what to say?*

'So, what do you think of the building?' Heidi mumbled.

'It's pretty impressive.'

Yes, it is. She wanted to say sarcastically, 'Which will no doubt make pretty impressive apartments' but she'd already decided she was going to keep her attitude in check, no matter what happened.

'Would you like something to drink?'

Vanessa nodded and Heidi gestured for her to follow her to the kitchenette.

'What do you fancy? Tea? Coffee?'

'A cold drink would be great if you have one.'

Heidi took out a carton of apple juice from the fridge and poured two glasses.

'You've got a lot of things stuffed in there,' Vanessa said, referring to the cramped fridge where the staff kept their lunches and drinks.

'Yeah,' Heidi said sheepishly, embarrassed by their meagre means. 'Joe's Appliances in King's Cross donated it to us.'

'When was this?'

'A few years back, when we were starting out.'

'It looks like it's seen better days,' Vanessa said. 'I can't imagine what it must be like in the summer getting hot and bothered without something cold to cool you down.'

Her words resonated around the room and Heidi stopped herself from giggling. She was meant to be projecting a professional image, not one of a love-sick teenager. Heidi cleared her throat. 'Would you like me to show you around?'

'Lead the way.'

'As I told your, ahem, brother yesterday, we offer workshops, one-on-one counselling in person as well as over the phone,' Heidi said, repeating the information she'd given Craig.

'I'm sorry things didn't go too well with my brother.'

Heidi wanted to tell her that Craig had been vulgar to the point of being abusive but she didn't want to start off on the wrong foot. She had experienced a huge paradigm shift. Her feelings hadn't changed towards Craig but they had about Vanessa.

'Don't worry about it. No harm done,' Heidi said as she guided Vanessa through the same route she'd taken Craig, only this time Vanessa engaged with everyone she was introduced to. She listened intently to the counsellors, chatted with the volunteers and generally took an interest in everything. Heidi couldn't believe the difference between the O'Neil siblings. More than ever, she was convinced they weren't blood relatives. *They can't be.*

Two hours later, they were back where they started. It struck Heidi that from the moment she had first laid eyes on Vanessa there had been a physical attraction. But now? It was so much more. In her heart she knew Vanesa really was the real deal. The whole package wrapped up into one beautiful parcel.

'Can you walk me downstairs?' Vanessa asked.

'Sure.'

Heidi tried to ignore the sinking feeling in the pit of her stomach as they neared the entrance. She didn't want Vanessa to leave. There was so much left unsaid.

As if she had read her mind Vanessa said, 'I know you must be wondering why I came.' They stopped at the bottom of the stairs. Vanessa turned to her and held her gaze. 'I feel really bad about this whole situation, but I know Craig. Once he's set his mind on something, he won't let go.'

'So we can't stay?'

'Not here, no. But I want to help you find another place.'

'You'd do that for us?' There was an awkward pause. 'Why?'

'Because I'm part of the problem. It's a family business—'

'But if it was up to you, would you evict us?'

'I think you already know the answer to that.'

'Say it.'

'No, I wouldn't evict you.'

Heidi's pulse raced. 'Why?'

Vanessa took a step closer. Her hand reached out, and her fingers lightly trailed the length of Heidi's arm. 'Because … I believe in what this place stands for.'

Goose pimples exploded at her touch. Instinctively, Heidi tilted her head upwards. She didn't know why. At that moment, she only knew that she wanted to be close to Vanessa in every way imaginable.

But it wasn't to be. Not yet anyway. Vanessa's phone rang. Shrill and loud in the quiet space between them. *Bloody mobile phones!*

Vanessa looked regretful as she withdrew her hand and walked backwards to the exit. 'I've got to take this. We'll speak soon.' She put the phone to her ear. 'Hi, Brett, I'll be there in ten.' And then she was gone.

Heidi stayed where she was for the moment, gazing at the empty spot where Vanessa had been standing just seconds before. The warmth of her touch still lingered and so did self-doubt. Heidi was alarmed at the territory her mind was drifting into. Had she read the signs correctly, was Vanessa interested? Or just a flirt?

With this thought in her mind, she walked to the door and inhaled a mouthful of air. Something moved in her peripheral vision and she quickly turned to see what it was.

'There she is again,' Heidi whispered under her breath.

The teenage girl she'd seen from her office window was again lurking in the shadow of the oak tree across the street. Heidi stepped outside onto the pavement and waved her hand in the air to catch her attention but the girl ignored Heidi's efforts. Before she could try again, the girl disappeared.

Chapter Fifteen

Vanessa made her way quickly to the cobbled alleyway beside the centre where she'd parked her car. *What was I thinking letting my guard down like that?* Her intention had been to make amends and ease the guilt a little, not end up in what could have been a compromising position. *Thank God Brett called when he did.*

She stuffed her hand in her pocket to retrieve her keys. *Heidi.* Vanessa could still feel the smoothness of her skin beneath her own. It had been a casual move on her behalf but there was nothing casual about the way her body had responded to Heidi's touch.

I obviously got too caught up in the moment. But it was okay, Vanessa was allowed a little flirtatious fun. The main thing was that she had fully recovered and her pulse had resumed its natural rhythm. All she needed to do was put the whole episode out of her mind. She would keep her word and follow through with her offer to help. As soon as she got back to the office she would ask Gina to look for office space for the charity to move into. Vanessa would cover the rent and tell Heidi by email that she'd found the charity a sponsor who wanted to pay for the property. Heidi's passion for her work not only touched Vanessa's heart but gave her renewed admiration for what she stood for. Vanessa had met women like Heidi before, who gave their time and energy for causes that made a big difference in people's lives. One day, in the future, Vanessa could see herself settling down with someone exactly like Heidi, but for now, she had to keep her distance. She didn't know what it was about Heidi that scared her but alarm bells rang so loudly they were hard to ignore.

As Vanessa got closer to her car, she narrowed her eyes. Something didn't look right. What's different? It wasn't the body work … It wasn't the ….

'What the?' Vanessa gasped in horror as her eyes dropped to the flat tyre. Moving quickly around the car she saw all four were flat. It was clear that the air hadn't just been let out of them. Whoever had done it meant to obliterate them entirely. Gashes stretched like coal-black smiles across the width of two of the tyres, while the other two displayed jagged rubber teeth where they'd been eviscerated by a crude tool.

It has to be someone from the centre trying to get back at me.

Seething, Vanessa hurried back to Heidi's office. She stopped at the reception desk and took a deep breath.

'Hey, you're back already?' Mel said.

'It would seem that way,' Vanessa said with a tight smile. 'Can you let Heidi know I'm here, please,' she said with as much composure as she could manage under the circumstances.

'Sure.' Mel picked up the phone and pressed a few buttons. 'Heidi. Vanessa O'Neil is here. Yes, of course I'm sure it's her. You introduced us, remember? Okay I'll tell her.' She hung up. 'She said to go up. Do you remember where her office is? If not, I can show you.'

'I'm sure I'll find it.' Vanessa started up the stairs. 'Thank you, Mel.'

Vanessa was grateful for the few minutes it took to get to Heidi's office. The last thing she wanted was for Heidi to see her as an unstable head case because her car had been vandalised. She wanted her to see her as everything her wretched brother was not. But boy, was it hard. Vanessa wasn't concerned about the cost of replacing the tyres, it was the fact that someone had targeted her specifically. All she had done was visit the centre to lend a helping hand and this is what she got in return.

'Vanessa?' Heidi said, rising from her seat when Vanessa entered her office. The smile on her face changed to one of concern. 'Is everything okay?'

'No, Heidi. It's not.'

'What's happened?'

Vanessa lowered herself onto an uncomfortable metal-framed seat. If she remained standing she might not be able to maintain her cool. 'Someone has vandalised my car. They slashed all of my tyres.'

'Slashed your tyres?' Heidi gasped. 'Who would do that?'

Vanessa raised her brows. 'Funnily enough, that's exactly what I asked myself.'

Heidi cocked her head. 'You don't think it was someone from here, do you?'

'Hmm, let's see,' Vanessa said, tapping her foot on the threadbare carpet. 'It's the first time I show up here and voila! My tyres are slashed. Do you think it was just a coincidence?'

Heidi let out a long sigh. 'I don't know. There's a lot of crime in this area, it could be—'

'I think we both know it was personal.'

'If it was, then I'm sorry.'

Vanessa saw the genuine sorrow in Heidi's eyes and her foul mood tapered off. *They're only wheels.* Nothing was worth making Heidi upset, especially something she had no control over. 'Can I use your phone to call the police? My battery's flat.'

'Of course, please,' Heidi said sympathetically and pushed the desk phone across the table to her.

'Thanks.' Vanessa called the police to report the incident, more for insurance purposes than for any real assistance in catching the perpetrator. Vanessa's eyes roamed over Heidi's slender body and mesmerising tresses as she walked away. Her gaze followed Heidi to the large window that overlooked the street.

After Vanessa finished the call, she crossed her legs, settling in for the long wait despite the officer assuring her someone would be out soon to take her statement. Once she had a crime number, she could contact her insurance company to arrange for her car to be towed.

Judging by the police's average response time for something not so urgent, she figured it would take until the end of the business day to get everything sorted out. The inconvenience drove her crazy.

'I feel so bad about this. Please let me pay for your tyres,' Heidi offered, taking a seat again.

Vanessa couldn't stop looking at her: the way her nose twitched when she was anxious, the way her pristine eyes glinted, the softness of her clear, silky voice.

'Vanessa?' Heidi repeated, catching Vanessa staring for a tad too long this time.

'Don't worry about the tyres.' When Heidi's eyebrows drew together Vanessa smiled. 'My insurance will cover it. But thanks for the offer.'

'No, I insist,' Heidi said. 'I feel terrible about the whole thing. If you hadn't come here, this wouldn't have happened.'

'Seriously, don't worry,' Vanessa said, but Heidi remained adamant to resolve the problem herself. It was at that moment that Vanessa realised what she found so attractive about Heidi. She was the type of person who took the world upon her shoulders to save or help others.

'What kind of car do you drive?' Heidi asked. She scooped up the receiver of her phone with one smooth movement and waited for Vanessa to answer. 'I need to know the make and model to get a quote.'

Knowing she could never afford the tyres, Vanessa gave a small shake of her head, hoping she wouldn't find her reaction patronising.

'Um … It's an Aston Martin DB11,' Vanessa said casually as if she were driving a Volkswagen Beetle. 'Make sure they quote you on the right diameter and tread depth.'

Heidi blinked a few times while the rest of her

body and face froze. Vanessa didn't want to laugh, but she looked as if she'd just gone into shock.

'An Aston Martin? Jesus, I could feed myself for a few months with one of those tyres,' she mumbled. Heidi replaced the handset and ran her fingers through her wild locks, showcasing the shape of her face and allowing Vanessa to appreciate the full picture of her beauty.

'Heidi, none of this is your fault, and you certainly don't have to pay for it.'

'But you'll want the police to investigate this as a crime, won't you? We don't even know if the person responsible is from here,' she said. 'I'd rather get a loan to cover the cost of the tyres than have police officers scaring people.'

Vanessa gave it some thought. Regrettably, the O'Neil way was usually opportunistic, to manipulate circumstances so that they were advantageous.

'I'll tell you what,' Vanessa said. 'If you let me take you out for something to eat, I'll forget about this whole thing. I won't get the police involved.'

Heidi tilted her head to one side, her expression caught between humour and distrust.

'Really?' she asked. 'I go out with you and that's it?'

Vanessa nodded. 'We're going to need to get a cab. You game?'

'Are you kidding? Of course. Forget the cab though. I've got a car. A very old Mini.'

'Does it have four wheels?'

'What?' Heidi laughed. 'Of course it does. When I said old I didn't mean it was a clapped out old banger.'

'Then it far exceeds my car, doesn't it?'

Vanessa called the police back and retracted her complaint, then phoned her local garage. She waited for Heidi to gather up her things.

'So, where are we going?' Heidi asked as she started the car.

'The South Bank,' Vanessa replied. 'There's a little place that does the best Mexican street food.'

'Great let's go.'

With a start, Vanessa realised she hadn't thought about work once the whole time she was in Heidi's company. She didn't know if it was a good thing or not.

Chapter Sixteen

Heidi drove through King's Cross and over Blackfriars Bridge, taking them into south London. The traffic, as always in rush hour, was bumper to bumper but Heidi didn't care how long they had to stay behind the BMW with the loud music blaring out of its window. She was in no rush now.

Vanessa smelt tantalising and her scent filled the inside of the small car. Heidi hoped it would seep into the fabric of the seats and remain long after she was gone.

Surprisingly, Heidi didn't feel nervous having Vanessa so close—excited maybe, but not nervous. She felt completely at ease in her company.

'They aren't bad kids at the centre you know,' Heidi said after a few minutes of silence.

'I didn't say they were.'

'I know, but your car—'

'I told you to forget about it.' Vanessa's hand touched her knee for a split second. It was enough to make Heidi want to reach across, slip her fingers through the gap in Vanessa's shirt and caress every inch of her. *What's happening to me?* Heidi had never been one to have so many sexual thoughts about a woman before they'd even been to bed together. If she was honest, she didn't usually think much about sex full stop.

The traffic started moving and it wasn't long

before they reached Waterloo.

'I can't believe it, there's a parking space,' Heidi said rushing to slot her car into the space before someone else beat her to it.

'Must be a sign,' Vanessa said.

A sign from God himself, or not, Heidi had to try and keep her wits about her. In her mind she was moving too fast. As much as she would have loved for it to be real, the truth was, she wasn't on a date with Vanessa. She had agreed to go out with her, not only to save the centre being visited by the police but to further explore the option of Vanessa helping them find a new space. It had absolutely nothing to do with her wanting to tear Vanessa's clothes off and get naked.

Both women exited the car simultaneously and made their way down the stairs to the embankment. Vanessa led the way to the Mexican restaurant and chose a table overlooking the river. They sat in silence as they studied the menu. Every few seconds Heidi glanced up to look at Vanessa and at one stage pinched her leg to make sure she wasn't dreaming. That she was actually sat opposite her. While they waited for their food and drinks to arrive, they made small talk about the design of the restaurant and the clever way it had been built using large steel storage containers to make dining areas.

'You surprise me,' Heidi said.

'Why's that?' Vanessa asked, before taking a bite of her burrito.

'This,' Heidi jerked her head to the building

around them. 'I didn't think you'd be into—'

'You think this is slumming it?' Vanessa asked with amusement.

'Oh no, not at all. Not for me anyway—'

'If it's good enough for you, why not me?'

'Because,' Heidi said awkwardly. 'You can afford to eat anywhere you like—'

'And I do. At places where the food is good. Are you enjoying your wrap?'

Heidi took a few seconds to savour the taste. 'It's amazing.'

'Well, there you go. It's nothing to do with money. I've eaten at Michelin star restaurants that have been … let's just say underwhelming. Money doesn't govern my choices in life.'

What must it be like to live like that? Money does nothing but govern my life.

'I'm sorry, I wasn't judging—'

'I didn't think you were.'

'It wasn't my intention, but I know I can sound a bit judgemental sometimes,' Heidi said.

'I like that you're straightforward.'

'You do?'

Vanessa nodded.

'Are you sure you're related to Craig? Because I still find it impossible to believe.'

'You're not the first and you won't be the last person to think that.'

Heidi took a mouthful of Coke. 'What was it like growing up with him?'

Vanessa considered the question carefully before answering. 'Difficult. Especially when he found out I was gay.'

'That bad huh?'

Vanessa shifted in her seat and lowered her eyes to her beer bottle, as if she was embarrassed to share any more personal information. So Heidi was surprised when Vanessa finally said, 'Worse than bad. I didn't need to come out to my parents, he did it for me. On their wedding anniversary in front of sixty guests. I thought my grandparents were going to drop dead on the spot.'

'Oh my God, what a ….' She paused abruptly. Heidi's expression must have shown her embarrassment, because Vanessa waved her hand dismissively, saving her from the obligation to continue.

'Prick,' Vanessa said. 'It's okay you can say it.'

'I was thinking something a little harsher. So, how did everyone take it?'

'Oh you know, a little embarrassed laugh here and there. Bless my dad, he opened his wine cellar and Craig's little speech was soon forgotten.'

'I don't know if I could have forgiven him after pulling a stunt like that.'

Vanessa took another swig of her beer, not bothering to hide her annoyance at the memory. 'When it's one thing after another, you soon forget what you were angry about in the first place.'

'And your parents? Do they let him get away with what he wants?'

'Both my parents are retired and live in Florida. My dad had a heart attack and my mum gave him an ultimatum. Divorce or retire. So he retired. He has nothing to do with the business anymore. My mum won't allow it.'

'So Craig's pretty much left to his own devices?' *What a scary thought.*

'Yeah you could say that. Most of the time I try to keep out of his way and his business dealings.' Vanessa stared at Heidi in such a way it made her stomach dance. 'Let's talk about you.'

Heidi shifted in her seat. 'Me?'

Vanessa nodded. 'Why would someone like you choose to work at the centre?'

'Why would someone like you choose to be a property developer?'

'I didn't have a choice.'

'Neither did I. My work at the centre is like a calling.'

'Sort of like a nun to the church?' Vanessa smiled.

'Yeah, you could say that. I remember how messed up I was when I was a teenager. The confusion, the wanting to belong, to be "normal" whatever that is. A place like Young Minds literally saved my sanity. So I suppose when the opportunity to manage the centre arose, I felt it was my chance to help others who were like me.'

'That makes sense.'

'Now you tell me something.'

'Whatever you want.'

As Vanessa's eyes roamed over Heidi's face the heat rose to Heidi's cheeks. How was it even possible for Vanessa to have that effect on her? Determined not to let her hormones get the better of her, she straightened in her seat and stared back at Vanessa, unblinking. Unwavering. *This would be so much easier if she wore sunglasses.* 'Did you tell your brother you were coming to the centre today?'

Vanessa shook her head and smiled.

'Why not?'

'Because what I do has got nothing to do with him. Besides, I think he's in the wrong.'

'For buying the property?'

'No, not that. Heidi, that property was put on the market ages ago. If it wasn't us that snapped it up, it would have been someone else. Howard Baker was determined to sell.'

What a little shit. 'Now that I didn't know.'

'It was the way Craig handled the situation I didn't agree with.'

'What, like letting us find out via social media? No, it wasn't very professional. So, what would he say if he found out about us doing—'

'Doing?'

'You know. This.'

'And what exactly is this?'

Something? Nothing? Heidi's chest tightened as Vanessa leant towards her.

'Do you mind if ….'

'No, no I don't.' Heidi's voice took on a husky

tone. Eyes closed, her lips formed a small pout. She counted the seconds, waiting for that first touch of her lips. Of Vanessa's soft sensuous mouth pressed against her own. In that moment, Heidi didn't care that they were sat outside, surrounded by a slew of commuters and tourists zipping past them. She didn't care about anything but … She frowned when a rough texture dabbed at her mouth.

Those aren't her lips. At least I hope they aren't.

Her eyes flew open in time to see Vanessa leaning back, paper napkin in hand. Heidi picked up her drink and sucked hard on the straw, trying to seem as if she hadn't been waiting in anticipation for an intimate moment. *Did I really think a successful business woman would snog me like a horny teenager? I need to get a grip.*

Heidi was grateful that Vanessa seemed more interested in the menu than her.

'That's the problem with this place. I can never have enough. Do you fancy something else?'

Heidi cleared her throat and held up her wrap half-heartedly. 'This is more than enough, thanks.'

'In that case, I think I'll have … The garlic ….' Vanessa stopped and glanced sideways at Heidi. A small smile played on her lips. 'Maybe not. I think I'll go with dessert instead. You?'

Heat rose all the way from Heidi's stomach, fanned out around her neck then crawled slowly to her face. 'Dessert sounds good. Thank you.'

Heidi broke the intense eye contact and glanced around at the other diners. They didn't seem to have a care in the world as they laughed and chatted amongst themselves. She turned back to Vanessa, who was still gazing at her through the thick lashes that framed her magnetic eyes.

'Are you seeing anyone?' Vanessa let the words trail off and took a mouthful of her drink.

'No, are you?' Heidi bit her bottom lip as she waited impatiently for her answer.

'No. Do you live alone?'

Heidi didn't know how long it would be before she would be forced to move into shared accommodation, but that wasn't the question. The sexy vixen sitting opposite wanted to know if there was somewhere they could be alone. Heidi nodded.

'Do you want to go back to your place?'

Vanessa shot her a look of such desire that Heidi wanted to climb over the table and kiss her delectable lips hard. Instead, she gripped the edge of her seat. *Yes, yes and yes.*

Vanessa's eyes flashed with amusement as if she sensed Heidi's inner yearning.

'Let's go then.'

The journey back to her apartment was made in silence. Heidi knew if she spoke she'd probably put her foot in it. What sane person would ask their potential lover if they were doing the right thing considering the circumstances? Instead of imagining Vanessa writhing beneath her in pure ecstasy all she saw in her mind's eye was Simone with a 'what the fuck' expression on her face. Or Richie eyeing her with distain and Christina, she didn't even want to think about what she'd say.

Heidi didn't want to act too hastily, which was a little late seeing as Vanessa was now standing in her living room, eyeing Heidi as if she was her first meal of the day.

'Coffee?' Heidi asked, hoping she hadn't missed any underwear lying around.

Vanessa shook her head and moved towards her, narrowing the gap between them with each step.

Fighting the urge to either flee or run straight into Vanessa's arms, Heidi said, 'How about some tea. Yes, tea's a good idea. Peppermint is great for the digestive system, especially after the meal we've just—'

Heidi stopped rambling when Vanessa was inches away. It was all too easy to get lost in Vanessa's gaze. She couldn't possibly pretend that she wasn't affected by her. Heidi's body pulsated in a way she had forgotten.

Vanessa reached out to Heidi, one hand firmly around her waist, the other gripping the back of her head. Heidi's spirits soared when Vanessa's body crushed against her own, her nipples so hard Heidi could feel them through the material of her shirt. Her heart thumped erratically. A low gasping moan escaped Heidi as Vanessa's tongue slid across Heidi's lips, then seductively slipped inside her mouth; tasting her, filling her, owning her. Lost in the euphoria of the moment, Heidi didn't prevent Vanessa's hand from moving up her skirt, skimming her thighs. Stroking, rubbing, probing. Melting inside her moist entrance. In a frenzy, Heidi's hands indiscriminately explored the silkiness of

Vanessa's thick hair, the firmness of her pert breasts, the length of her toned back. Now she was kissing back hard. Heidi desperately wanted to rip the clothes from Vanessa's body, drag her into the bedroom and devour each and every part of her body. Inch, by inch.

Suddenly, reality hit home and Heidi started thinking about what the consequences would be if things went any further. Yes, they would end up having mind-blowing sex, but then what? Vanessa would no doubt leave, having considered their encounter to be nothing more than a one-night stand. Heidi would be heartbroken and downtrodden, *again*. And there was always the chance of Vanessa back-tracking on her decision to help the centre, deciding it wasn't such a good move to mix business with pleasure. The end result would leave the centre in an even worst position and it would all be because Heidi couldn't keep her fantasy where it should be. In her head.

The choice of having support for the centre or having hot sex was staring her straight in the face, but she knew there wasn't a chance in hell she could have both. One had to go.

'Wait,' Heidi barely managed to say. Her mouth still tingled in the aftermath of Vanessa's fiery embrace.

'Don't stop, not now.'

'I … We can't do this … Not yet,' Heidi said breathlessly, reluctantly pushing Vanessa's hand away. 'I'm not ready for this.'

Vanessa's heavy, hooded eyes burnt with desire. 'You could have fooled me.'

Heidi took a step back and instinctively crossed her arms, creating a barrier between them. 'I want this so badly—'

'But?'

'It doesn't feel right … I mean it does feel right. It's amazing,' she said flustered. 'Just not now.'

'You're right.' Vanessa quickly buttoned her shirt as she spoke. 'We're moving too fast.'

'Only because of the circumstances.' Heidi's voice was full of regret at the lost opportunity. She couldn't believe how close she had come to having sex for the first time in over a year. Stifling a sigh and trying to ignore a surge of frustration, she forced herself to say something. 'Do you fancy a tea?'

'No.'

'Are you sure because—'

'It's late. Would you mind calling me a cab please?'

Heidi swallowed her disappointment. 'A cab? Yeah okay.'

Palms slick with sweat, Heidi fished her phone out of her pocket and called the local taxi firm. 'It'll be here in five minutes,' she said as she hung up.

'Thanks.' Vanessa hesitated, her eyes unreadable. 'I think I'll wait downstairs.'

'Are you sure?'

Vanessa nodded.

'Okay,' Heidi said, even though she knew things weren't okay between them. Not now that the line between their professional and personal lives had become blurred.

'I enjoyed tonight,' Vanessa said.

'Me too, I only wish—'

'You don't have to explain.'

Vanessa walked out of the door, leaving Heidi to wonder how long it would be before she saw her again and what, if anything, would happen between them.

Chapter Seventeen

Vanessa had been lost, *smitten*, from the very first moment she laid eyes on Heidi. Not that she would ever admit it, *especially to Natalie*. Even in her mind the thought sounded like a distasteful confession. How could she own up to something when she didn't even know what she wanted from Heidi. Sex? Most definitely. But she knew being involved with a woman like Heidi was never going to be a 'jump in, jump out' type of affair and, no matter how much Vanessa tried to convince herself that she could take or leave her, Heidi had got under her skin. Every part of her body still pulsated, yearned with an ache not yet satisfied. Vanessa might look like a controlled woman on the outside, but tonight her insides were a burning inferno. Nobody had ever elicited emotions like Heidi had, and this knowledge disturbed her on many levels.

But what's the point of feeling like this? Vanessa knew it could never go any further. Not when her home life was so complicated. She had Kelli to think about. *And I'm hardly doing a great job on that front.*

Kelli's thunderous voice played in her head. *I wish you had died instead of my mother.*

The last thing Vanessa wanted was to provide Kelli with yet another reason to hate her. If she suddenly appeared to be happily dating, it would be like rubbing salt in an open wound. It would unsettle Kelli and make her feel like she was a burden to Vanessa, even though this was the furthest thing from the truth.

And then there was Craig. Despite her growing hatred of the man he had become, he was family, and that meant sticking together. Facing the world as one. She couldn't betray him, regardless of how much he deserved it. Her loyalty to the family came first and always would.

Whichever way she turned, it seemed her happiness would be denied.

Arriving home, Vanessa went straight to her bedroom. She wanted to be alone with her thoughts … *Heidi.* No matter how hard she tried to fight it, she knew it was futile trying to forget those few minutes of bliss.

Vanessa crossed the room and closed the blinds, before turning off her bedside lamp. She slipped out of her clothes, letting them drop to the floor, and slid into bed. The sheets were cool against her heated body as she closed her eyes and soon drifted. In a semi-conscious state, she imagined she was still in Heidi's apartment, feeling the vibration of Heidi's hypnotic heart beat pounding against her chest, her arms draped around Heidi's neck pulling her close. Her hand seared a path down Heidi's stomach and along her inner thigh, until she reached her swollen clit. Every thought of her earlier encounter with Heidi, made Vanessa's body quiver with need. The aroused pink tip of Heidi's breast, the wetness between her legs. Vanessa's lips parted and she could all but taste the sweetness of Heidi's mouth.

She drew in a short sharp breath, shocked by the

intensity of her imagination. When her hand located the throbbing spot it sought, she quickened her circular movement as fire spread throughout her. In her mind's eye, she saw Heidi's naked body sprawled out beneath her own; waiting, wanting. Vanessa bit her lip as Heidi's face became more vivid. Her breasts rose sharply as she drew in jagged breaths. Her aroused nipples shivered. Flushed by a dizzying rush of emotion, the last shuddering moments came upon her. Now the flame-like urgency had passed, with Heidi still occupying her mind, Vanessa relaxed and let ripple upon ripple of ecstasy seep through her entire body. *It might not have happened today, but it will happen—and soon. Business deal or not.* That was one guarantee Vanessa could give her.

Chapter Eighteen

What's the worst that can happen?

Kelli had been asking herself the same question for over an hour and she still hadn't come up with a suitable reply. She'd been standing around like a wallflower, working up the nerve to go inside the centre. In the end, she resorted to drinking the can of beer she had stashed in her bag for emergencies. Kelli didn't have a drink problem per se; she just used alcohol to ease the sorrow from eating into her soul. It actually helped her feel something. Even if it was undiluted rage at the unfair hand she had been dealt in her short life. She would gladly hang on to an emotion to make her feel human.

Popping a piece of chewing gum into her mouth, Kelli chomped furiously. *Come on, you can do it. You just need to take a few steps.* As if on command, her legs soon carried her across the road, stopping feet away from the entrance of the centre. She blew a mouthful of breath into her cupped hands to make sure the scent of alcohol had been masked.

Butterflies danced in her stomach as Kelli pulled open the door and stepped over the threshold. *I did it, I did it. I'm here.*

The woman standing behind the reception desk glanced over at her. She was blonde with out of control, frizzy hair and gave Kelli a welcoming smile. Kelli's shoulders relaxed a little.

'Hello?' the woman tilted her head to one side, waiting for Kelli to complete the sentence with her name.

Kelli said the first name that came to mind. 'Mandy.'

'Hi, Mandy. Come in.'

Kelli took one step forward and stopped, like a frightened animal unsure of her intentions.

'I don't bite.' Her soft tone put Kelli at ease.

'Is Christina around?' Kelli inched a few feet closer, her confidence growing with each step.

'Christina? I saw her milling around earlier, I'll just check.'

If the woman was surprised that Kelli knew someone at the centre, her expression didn't show it. Kelli stuffed her hands in her jacket pockets as the woman picked up the phone.

'Simone, it's Mel. Can you ask Christina to come to reception please? She has a visitor.'

In that instant, Kelli wanted to turn and run as far away from the centre as possible. She wasn't ready to see Christina again. Not now. *What was I thinking?* It was too late. Christina was on her way down the stairs.

'You came!' Christina beamed as she jumped from the second step and strode over to Kelli.

Kelli took a step back, wary Christina might try and hug her. She couldn't risk Christina feeling her body tremble. Folding her arms across her chest she said simply, 'Yeah.'

'Do you want to come upstairs or go for a walk?'

'A walk,' Kelli muttered. *Breathe.* Just being in the same space as Christina was a big enough step for one day.

'A walk it is.' Christina turned to face Mel. 'I've got my phone if anyone needs me.'

Christina opened the door and gestured for Kelli to leave first. Soon they were walking in the direction of the small park a few minutes away.

'So, you got a name?' Christina asked as they walked into the play area.

Kelli grabbed hold of a swing and sat down. She thought about keeping up her charade of being Mandy but didn't see the point. It was only a name and if she wanted to get to know Christina better she'd find out sooner or later. 'Kelli.'

'Nice to meet you, Kelli.'

Christina stood in front of her and held out her hand. This time Kelli took it. Christina smiled before dropping onto the swing next to hers.

Using the balls of their feet, they pushed themselves back and forth in a comfortable silence. Every now and again, Kelli gave Christina a sideways glance and her stomach flipped over. She looked so content, peaceful—a state of being Kelli could only dream of.

'So what do you do at the centre?' Kelli asked, genuinely interested to find out more about her.

'I just help out. Do admin, and whatever else needs doing.'

'Do you ever talk to ….' The words wouldn't come

out. She'd never dared speak them out loud before.

'Do I talk to people like you?' Christina finished for her, in a voice laced with compassion and understanding.

'And who are people like me?' Kelli wanted the truth to come from Christina's lips, not her own.

'People who feel confused and have no one to turn to.'

'And why don't they have anyone to talk to?' Kelli pressed, relieved to know it wasn't just her that felt this way.

Christina shrugged. 'Because they're scared of rejection, ridicule, of people hating them for being different.'

Kelli remained silent for a few minutes before she spoke again. 'How did you know? About me, I mean?'

Christina grabbed the chain on Kelli's swing, bringing her to an abrupt halt. Kelli kept her gaze straight ahead.

'Because I used to have that same look when I first came to London.' Christina got to her feet and stood in front of Kelli again. 'There's nothing wrong with you. I know it's hard at first but once you come to terms with being gay, it does get easier. Accepting who you are I mean.'

There. Christina had said the dreaded word and Kelli's world hadn't come crashing down on her. Lightning hadn't struck her dead. She was still the same person she'd been only seconds ago.

'Have you told anyone? Family? Friends?'

Kelli shook her head, tears welling up in her eyes.

'You know you'd be surprised to learn how many people you love aren't raging homophobes. Sometimes I think we just punish ourselves because it's us who can't accept the truth.'

Kelli nodded, not trusting herself to speak. The last thing she wanted to do was start blubbering on a child's swing like a baby, but the relief of admitting her true feelings to someone proved too much and tears rolled down her cheeks.

She hadn't told Vanessa the truth because she knew she wouldn't believe her. She'd put it down to Kelli being an attention seeker, wanting to be different for the sake of it.

Christina gave Kelli's shoulder a reassuring squeeze. Her touch caused a tingling sensation to spread from her head to her toes. Kelli closed her eyes briefly to savour the moment and felt the darkness around her world evaporate.

'Listen, let me set you up with one of the counsellors at the centre. They really helped me and they will do the same for you,' Christina said.

Kelli smiled. 'Okay, thanks.'

They stayed in the park talking until the blue sky darkened. Kelli told Christina everything about her, except that she was related to Vanessa. She didn't want the door slammed in her face before Christina realised she was nothing like her aunt. Before she had the chance to kiss her.

When Kelli's phone vibrated in her pocket, she

knew it would be Vanessa demanding to know where she was. That was one conversation she didn't want to have in front of Christina. She discreetly turned it off instead of answering it.

'I'd better go,' Kelli said reluctantly as she rose to her feet.

Sadness flickered in Christina's eyes.

'Do you want to swap numbers?' Christina asked. 'The centre might be closing down soon, so I don't know how much longer I'll be volunteering there.'

'I wouldn't be too worried.' Kelli slung her rucksack over her shoulder and made off towards the park's entrance. 'I'm gonna help you in any way I can. Trust me.'

She gave Christina one last wave before running to the train station.

Chapter Nineteen

For the first time in forever, Heidi awoke feeling revitalised. Not to mention randy as hell. Vanessa had awoken something in her that had lain dormant for years, and she liked it. No, loved it. Feeling desired made all the difference to a mundane Friday morning.

Heidi shrugged off the voice telling her not to get too carried away with the notion that last night was the beginning of something special. A dark premonition clouded the back of her mind but she wrote it off. Her past tribulations were due to her negative mindset and the expectation that things were going to go wrong. But after last night, things were on the up and she refused to sabotage her happiness anymore.

Even the weather seemed to be playing along. For the spring season, the morning was remarkably warm and the blue sky was cloud-free. As Heidi pulled on her knee-length boots, she inadvertently cast a glance at the space where she had stood with Vanessa the night before. She could still feel Vanessa's confident touch, and she revelled in the deep kiss they'd shared just before Vanessa slid her hand up her dress and … *Oh how different things could have been if I didn't have a conscience.* She shook her head, banishing the 'what ifs' from her mind. *You did the right thing.* Oddly enough, they hadn't even exchanged numbers. *I wonder if she would have sent me a sexy text message this morning if we had?*

Heidi hoped that Vanessa would show up at the centre today, even if it was under the guise of trying to figure out how they were going to find another property. Once that was done, they could go for a drink and pick up where they left off. With that in mind, Heidi wore her sexiest top; a black cashmere V-neck that stopped just short of her cleavage. Stylish with a touch of class.

Heidi left her flat and crossed the road to her car on the other side, hoping Vanessa's perfume still permeated the inside. She wasn't disappointed. The scent was strong enough for Heidi to imagine Vanessa sitting beside her for the twenty-minute drive to work.

As soon as she opened the door to the centre she switched from lovey-dovey-school-girl-crush mode to professional, the captain of a condemned vessel.

I've got to act normally. It was Simone she had to avoid. One look in Heidi's eyes and it would be game over. Simone would know someone had lit Heidi's fire.

Reaching the top of the stairs, she knew something was wrong. The normal buzz in the centre wasn't there for a start. *In fact, where is everyone?*

Heidi passed Simone's vacant room as she headed to her office.

As she tossed her bag into the desk's bottom drawer, Christina's voice sounded from behind her. 'Heidi.'

'Morning, Chris. Where is everyone?' Heidi asked cheerfully.

Christina tried to hide her sullen mood but she

failed terribly. 'What's wrong?'

Christina ignored her question. 'Can you please come to the conference room? We need to talk to you about something.'

We? Heidi's stomach sank like it did when she was a child being summoned to the head teacher's office. She was in trouble but she couldn't imagine what for.

Walking into the conference room felt like entering a sea of negative emotion. Her colleagues were sat at the table, grimacing at her. The once smiling, happy-go-lucky people she knew like family now resembled a firing squad.

'If this is an inquisition, I'm innocent,' she mock pleaded.

'Thanks for nothing, Heidi,' Simone said coldly.

Simone sat in Heidi's usual seat at the head of the table so Heidi took the only available chair. Simone slid a food menu across the polished desk to her. A shot of betrayal struck deep in Heidi's core, escaping in an audible gasp.

'We know you and Vanessa went out together last night,' Simone said in her coldest voice.

'What are you talking about?' Heidi asked, astonished. *How the hell could they have found out?*

'Oh come on, Heidi. You're not going to deny it are you?' Richie jumped in, his hands folded between his knees, his face scrutinising her inquiry. 'We have proof.'

'Proof?'

'Yes proof,' Simone said, sliding an A4 sized

envelope across the table to her.

Heidi picked it up and peeked inside. 'What's this?'

'You tell us,' Simone said.

Heidi's fingers fished inside and pulled out several photographs. The first was of Vanessa and herself at the restaurant. She dropped them onto the table as if they had scorched her fingers and swallowed the bile that had crept up her throat. She straightened her back in an attempt to compose herself. 'Where did they come from?'

'They were delivered this morning, and it's a good thing they were, otherwise we'd be none the wiser that you're a turncoat,' Simone said.

'A what? Are you serious?'

'The pictures speak for themselves, Heidi.' Richie stared at her with disgust. 'You look pretty cosy with the person evicting us.'

Heidi glanced down at the photos again and there was no denying it. They did look like a couple on a first date. If it wasn't so scary that someone had followed them, it would have been quite cute.

'It's pretty obvious you weren't with her trying to save the centre,' Christina said.

'And that spells only one thing,' Mel added. 'You're in cahoots with them, probably siding with them for when the doors close on us and you need a new job.'

Oh God, can this get any worse?

'Did she happen to tell you that she was going to blackmail you—'

'Blackmail?'

'Yes.' Mel handed her a piece of paper. 'If you keep fighting the eviction, the pictures of you two will be released to the press. Which means we haven't got a leg to stand on.'

'Oh Christ, is this for real?' Heidi's voice rose unintentionally as she scanned the letter. 'This is bullshit. I'm as shocked as you. I had a business dinner with Vanessa. If anything—'

'Give it up, Heidi. We know something's going on between the two of you,' Simone said, shaking her head. 'There's a photo of you both entering your building.'

'I did not sleep with her if that's what you're getting at,' Heidi retorted, 'Nothing ....' she paused. She couldn't outright lie, but that didn't mean she couldn't be economical with the truth. 'Look it's true, we went out and, before you start getting your knickers in a twist, she said she was going to help us.'

Simone cocked her head. 'And is she? Going to help us—'

'Or just you?' Mel chimed in.

'You lot really are taking the piss now. How dare you question my loyalty to this place and to you.' Heidi looked around and took the time to stare at each one of them individually. 'And for what? To be fucking broke and soon to be homeless.'

Her colleagues caught their breath. If they wanted to make her out to be a traitorous bitch, the gloves were coming off. She picked up the letter and shook it in her fist.

'I went out for a meal in the hope of getting Vanessa to talk her brother round, nothing else.' Her voice was fully raised now. She was done trying to be all things to everyone, only to be shat on from a high place. 'And I am tired of people hanging me out to dry despite me trying my hardest to save this place, regardless of the personal cost to me. You want to know where we stand? I'll go and find out, shall I? Once and for all and then you can all go back into your glass houses—'

'Heidi—'

'Don't, Simone. Just don't. You of all people.' Heidi scrunched the letter into a ball and threw it on the table. Her eyes welled with tears and she roughly brushed them away with the back of her hand. 'I thought you were better than this.'

Heidi pushed her chair back roughly and stormed towards the door.

'Wait! Where are you going?' Harry asked.

She spun around with force, nearly spraining her neck. 'Berkley O'Neil is about to get a visit from me. I'm done playing nice. With everyone, including you lot.'

***

Not even the icy droplets of rain were enough to douse Heidi's fiery mood as she stormed into Vanessa's office building. She was actually dizzy with rage. No, rage was an understatement. She was furious to have been put on the spot like that. It wouldn't have been so bad if

Simone had asked to have a quiet word with her in the privacy of her office. Heidi would have told her the truth because that's what friends did. They didn't ambush you and humiliate you in front of your colleagues.

By the time she reached the reception desk, the look on Heidi's face must have been enough to send warning signals to Liz not to mess with her.

Heidi drummed her fingers on her desk while Liz called up to Vanessa's office. She'd already decided her plan of action if Vanessa refused to see her. She was going up anyway, even if it meant having the security guards chasing her. She would search for Vanessa floor by floor until she found her.

Thankfully that wasn't going to be necessary.

'You can go right up. Twelfth floor.'

'Thank you,' Heidi said through gritted teeth.

The annoying pop music in the lift did little to mellow her mood, instead it only served to fuel her anger further. The doors opened and Heidi caught sight of Vanessa through her glass walled office. She looked beautiful, regal and poised, even just sat at her desk deep in thought. For a second Heidi forgot she was angry and was instead overcome with mixed emotions. She really liked her, more than she could have imagined, and it pained her to think that Vanessa had somehow tricked her into deceiving her colleagues. That the whole point of going out together had been a ruse. A photo opportunity to make it look like it was more than just an innocent dinner. *Until we were behind closed doors. Stop thinking about her like that. She's not who you think she is. It's because of her that the centre's going to be closed down.*

As if sensing her presence, Vanessa swivelled round in her chair. Their eyes met. Neither woman smiled. This was for real. *Forget all about love and romance.* Heidi was going to tell Vanessa exactly what she thought of her and her vile brother.

'Heidi,' Vanessa addressed her with a guarded expression.

'Before you start with any nonsense about how you didn't know—'

'Hold on a second, know about what?'

'You're a good actress, I'll give you that much.'

Heidi got it. She really did. The reason why Vanessa would trick Heidi into thinking she was on her side. It was all about profit and family loyalty. High stakes. But that didn't mean it didn't hurt, bad. If only Heidi had read the warning signs she wouldn't be here in this office right now, about to blow a gasket. It could have been prevented if she would have only been more vigilant. She wanted to talk about it. Needed to hear Vanessa say it out loud. *That I'm a gullible fool.* No matter how unbearable it was.

'Heidi—'

'And last night.' Heidi paused. 'I guess that was an act as well.'

Vanessa rose from her desk and quickly moved to close the door. 'Do you mind if we start—'

'That's what I've come here to tell you, Vanessa. There is no us and there never will be.' Her voice faltered as she forced the words out. The words that her heart begged her not to say.

'Look, if it's about yesterday, I'm sorry—'

'Whatever we did or didn't have yesterday is a world apart from what we have now. I thought you were decent. That you understood the centre's plight—'

'I did, I do.'

'Really? Is that why you had us followed?' Heidi threw the accusation at her with casual disgust.

'What are you talking about? Who followed us?'

A frown deepened on Heidi's forehead. Does she really not know? The need to believe her was overwhelming but the trust she once had for her was now a thing of the past. She was well aware that Vanessa was a smooth talker. That she could cast you under her spell within minutes of being in her presence. Heidi should know. Hadn't she fallen under it herself. *And I stupidly believed she wanted to help*. When Heidi spoke, her words were flat. Weak. Even to her own ears. 'It doesn't matter—'

'Well, it obviously does to you.'

'What's the point?' Heidi closed her eyes briefly to block out the sight of Vanessa, but even when she did, she could still see the image burnt into her mind. The one of them in an intimate embrace. The memory was no longer pure. It was tainted with betrayal. *I don't want to hear any more lies. Not from her.* 'You'll just deny it.'

'Try me.'

Heidi's arms automatically tightened across her chest. 'The photos, Vanessa. Of you and me that were delivered to the centre this morning.'

'You've got to believe me—'

'And I suppose you know nothing of the letter threatening to make them public if I oppose the eviction?'

Vanessa walked over to her window and kept her back to Heidi. This dismissive action only served to wind Heidi up further.

'Is this why you asked me out last night? To set me up? I can't believe I nearly gave into you,' Heidi said, hating herself for opening up to Vanessa and letting her into her life and her heart.

A look of resignation shone in Vanessa's eyes. 'Heidi, listen—'

'No, I'm done listening. My first instinct was right, you're no better than your wacko brother.'

Vanessa turned. 'I am—'

'You see that's the problem, Vanessa. You're not. No matter how hard you try to fight it, you're both cut from the same cloth. Greed and the need to be top dog is inherent in you both—'

'Sit down, let's talk about—'

'What, so you can lie to me again?'

'Heidi, I didn't lie to you. I said I'd help you find a new building. That's all. Nothing more.'

'Nothing more?' Heidi almost yelled. The anger that coursed through her veins wasn't all about Vanessa; it had more to do with her colleagues at the centre. It hurt they thought so little of her, and Vanessa would be the one paying for their disloyalty.

Heidi couldn't ignore the sinking feeling in her stomach as she said, 'I wouldn't be surprised if you were the one who came up with the idea in the first place. Seduce the love-struck idiot.' *Oops. I shouldn't have said that.*

Vanessa's nostrils flared slightly. 'Do you really believe that?'

'What else am I to believe? It's all "divide and conquer" with businesses like yours, isn't it? Well, you were a great success. My colleagues think I sold them out—'

'Heidi—'

'Don't Heidi me. I've got your number, Vanessa O'Neil. You ain't gonna charm your way out of this one.'

Vanessa walked back to her desk and sat down, seemingly unfazed by Heidi's outburst. When she spoke, a cold edge tinged her voice. 'I think we're done here, don't you?'

'At least we agree on something.' Heidi made to leave, then stopped. 'You might be too spineless to go up against your brother, but I'm not.'

Chapter Twenty

It was hard for Vanessa to know how to react to Heidi's accusations. The calm and collected woman she spent time with yesterday now looked like she was falling apart. *The stress must be really getting to her if she thinks I set up a fake date to make her look bad.*

Vanessa's first reaction was to follow her but she thought that would be pointless. Nothing was going to get through to Heidi in the state she was in. If she was going to be angry with anyone she should have directed her outburst towards Craig, after all he was the one who was responsible for the dilemma she was in. Vanessa picked up her phone with every intention of giving Craig a piece of her mind when he strolled in looking like the happiest man in the world. Vanessa replaced the handset and looked up at him through narrowed eyes.

'I take it that was that Cross woman,' he said with a self-satisfied smirk.

'You don't look surprised she was here.'

'Nope.' He dropped onto the seat opposite her and put his feet up on her desk.

Vanessa leant over and brushed them off. 'What do you mean, nope? Is that because you had us followed?'

'Maybe.'

'What the hell does maybe mean? Either you did or you didn't.' Vanessa didn't know why she bothered to ask. She knew the answer. It wouldn't be the first time

Craig did something underhanded. His reputation was built on it. No doubt he had sought revenge against Heidi for rebuking his advances and now it seemed he had achieved it.

'Would I lie to you?'

'Do I need to answer that?'

'No, little sister, I wouldn't lie to you.'

'So, you didn't have us followed?'

'I didn't say that.'

'Will you stop playing childish games and tell me the truth?'

'All right, you nagging women are enough to give a man a stroke. Yes, I had you followed—'

'Why would you do something like that?'

'Because I knew you'd both play into my hands. It was only a matter of time.'

'Play into your hands? What are you talking about?'

'Don't be coy, Nessie. Did you think I didn't see the way you looked at her when she gave her first press conference? I'd have had to be blind to have missed it.'

Vanessa busied herself with paperwork on her desk to buy herself time. *Am I really that transparent?* 'Whatever you think you saw, doesn't give you the right—'

'That's where you're wrong. Protecting this company gives me every right to do what the fuck I want—'

'And that includes blackmail?'

'Oh, she told you about that then.' He grinned as he crossed his leg over his knee and sank back in his seat. 'I thought that was quite an ingenious move on my part.'

'You're sick, do you know that? This vendetta you've got has nothing to do with protecting the company. You want to destroy Heidi because she hurt your frail ego.'

'No one, and I mean no one, gets one over me. If you two weren't so fucking predictable I wouldn't have been able to get the goods on her. To be honest, I thought it would take longer than a day for you to get in her pants—'

'I didn't sleep with her.'

'You know, I actually believe you. She strikes me as the frigid type so I knew you'd be right in there. Anything for a challenge, eh?'

For the hundredth time that day she found herself wishing Craig would just disappear. Vanish from her life forever. 'Your arrogance is going to catch up with you one of these days.'

'Not before I own all of London.'

'Oh, I think it will a lot sooner than that.'

He looked uneasy. 'Meaning?'

'Meaning, you've poked the hornet's nest this time so you better get ready for the consequences.'

'From the dyke? Don't make me laugh. She doesn't scare me.'

'I'm sure she doesn't but public opinion should. If she gets them on side, you can kiss your project goodbye.'

'You'd love that, wouldn't you? So you could go play happy dykes with her. Well, you can put that dream to bed. By the time I'm finished with her, she's never going to want to be near an O'Neil again.'

With that, he left her office. Her head spun as she wondered what Craig had in store for Heidi next. Again, torn by loyalty to the family name, Vanessa considered calling her father, but shot that idea down immediately. The doctor had been stern about his advice—no stress.

Who else do I have to turn to? The board? She knew there wasn't a chance in hell that they'd side with her. They were in the business to make money, plain and simple.

The thought of being stuck in the middle of Heidi and Craig had proved too much. Vanessa wasn't one to thrive on drama and that is exactly what the whole episode had become. From today, she decided, she was going to wash her hands of the project and let them get on with it.

Desperate for something safe to occupy her mind, Vanessa put on her reading glasses and went back to work. All memories of Heidi were pushed firmly out of her mind.

***

Without a football match to draw a crowd, the pub was quieter than usual. A few men milled around the bar area drinking pints, while the barman was engrossed in something on his phone. Natalie was already seated at a table when Vanessa caught sight of her. *My saviour.* If Vanessa had arranged the evening with anyone else but Natalie, she would have cancelled. She felt emotionally drained and didn't have the energy to put on social graces with anyone else.

It was a strange situation she found herself in. Despite the initial flurry of enthusiasm for her work project, Vanessa had spent most of the day thinking about Heidi and the effect she was having on her life. She had tried to erase her from her thoughts after the episode in her office, but found it near enough impossible.

'Sorry I'm late,' Vanessa said, giving Natalie a long hug.

'You're not. I'm early. After the day I've had, I need this,' Natalie said, picking up the bottle of white wine and pouring Vanessa a glass.

'That bad, huh?'

'Worse.' Natalie rolled her eyes. 'Angela moved back in.'

Vanessa dropped her bag on the floor and slumped onto the empty chair next to her. 'What? Why?' Vanessa asked, confused. 'I thought—'

Natalie held up her hands in defeat. 'I know, I know. She's still a hormonal cow, but … and this is the problem, the make-up sex is so damn good.'

'So why the sour face?'

'Because it only hits me when we're not having hot and sweaty sex, that we're so much better apart. Oh, Nessie, tell me what to do,' she pleaded like a child.

Vanessa took a sip of her wine, savouring its crisp freshness. 'Believe me, I'm the last person you want advice from.'

Natalie pouted. 'That's not true. You always know what's best for me, even before I do.'

'I wish I could say the same for myself,' she said miserably.

'Aww what's up?' Natalie draped her arm around Vanessa's hunched shoulders.

'I've just had a shitty day.'

'Someone upset you?'

Was Vanessa actually upset or just pissed off with the situation she found herself in? In hindsight, Vanessa accepted the fact that Heidi had every right to be angry. What she didn't accept was being made the scapegoat. Why was she the one who always got caught in the crossfire? She shrugged, more so for the thoughts running through her mind than Natalie's question. 'Heidi—'

Natalie barely gave her the chance to utter another word before she interrupted her.

'Oh my God, I knew it.' Natalie shuffled her seat closer to Vanessa's. 'Come on, tell all you sly fox.'

Vanessa ran the tip of her finger along the stem of her glass. 'I only wanted to take her out for a drink—'

'Whoa, forget the boring part,' Natalie said rubbing her hands together in glee. 'Get straight to the juicy bits.'

Vanessa gave a short laugh. That was Natalie all over, straight to the main event; forget any chance of titillating foreplay. 'Okay. So I went back to her place.'

'And?' Natalie pressed excitedly.

'And,' Vanessa looked upwards as the memory washed over her, 'we kissed.'

'What! I knew it, I knew it.' Natalie propped her elbows on the table and rested her chin on her open palms. 'So, what was she like? On a scale of one to ten.'

'As a kisser? Hmm,' Vanessa said thoughtfully as she imagined Heidi's beautifully shaped lips. 'Definitely a plus ten.'

'Nice one!' Natalie had a wild gleam in her eyes. The one she always got whenever she thought or talked about sex. 'And in the sack?'

'We didn't actually get that far.'

'What?' Natalie gave her a sceptical look and sank back in her chair. 'That's so lame. Why would you let an opportunity like that pass you by? Are you crazy?'

'It wasn't me. Heidi didn't want things to go that far. She thought it was best not to muddy the waters.'

'Beautiful and sensible,' Natalie said, topping up her own glass before taking a sip. 'Not a good combination if you want to get your leg over.'

'Tell me about it.'

'Are you going to see her again?'

'Doubt it. I think she sees me as the number one enemy now.'

'Now?'

'Oh, I didn't tell you, Craig had us followed.'

Natalie pulled a face. 'Is he for real?'

'Afraid so. He had someone take pictures of us together, which he is now trying to blackmail her with.'

Natalie stared at her with a slight tilt of her head. 'Sorry, babe, but he is one sick fucker. Your own brother?'

'I know. I don't even know why I was surprised. Anyway, Heidi came to my office and had another go at me, accusing me of all sorts.'

'Why you?'

'Apparently, I'm in cahoots with Craig.'

'I hope you put her right.'

'To be honest, I didn't know what she was going on about. By the time Craig admitted it, it was too late.'

'Then why haven't you told her the truth?'

'I don't know if I can be bothered with all the drama.'

'Drama caused by your brother,' Natalie reminded her with a wry smile. 'I think I'd be pissed off as well if he had someone follow me.'

'It's not just that. She frightens me.'

Natalie's forehead creased in confusion. 'In what way?'

'I don't know.' An intense feeling of uneasiness came over Vanessa, causing her to shift her gaze to the window. 'When I'm with her I can't think of anything but her and when I'm not with her—'

'You're still thinking of her,' Natalie finished for Vanessa. Her voice had an undertone of understanding. 'And that's a bad thing because?'

'I'm not ready for anything deep at the moment.'

'I'm sorry to be the one to point this out to you, but you're thirty now—'

'Thanks for reminding me.'

'Which means it's time for you to stop acting like a hormonal teenager. Do you want to be alone forever?'

'Of course not, but—'

Natalie laughed. 'Why is there always a "but" with you? I've noticed you never use that word when you talk about work, yet as soon as things become too personal "but" is in most of your sentences.'

'Only because I know my work inside out; the workings of another woman's mind, I don't.'

'Well there's only one way to figure it out. Get your arse round to her place—'

Vanessa looked at her blankly. 'But—'

'Shhh, you're doing it again. Just go.'

'What about you?'

Natalie tapped her wine glass and smiled. 'I have all that I need right here. Now shoo. Go, and keep me updated.'

Vanessa drained the rest of her wine in one gulp. 'I hope I'm not going to regret this.'

Natalie took on the expression of a wise owl. 'In this life, you can only regret the things you never got to do. Don't let this be one of them. Now go.'

Chapter Twenty-One

Heidi was too wound up to return to work after her showdown with Vanessa. Instead she went home, where she could curl up and lick her wounds before she had to face the world again. As always, Vanessa dominated her thoughts. *Does she really think I'm that naïve? That I would believe her protests of innocence?* Love sick she might have been, but a fool? Never.

If Vanessa wasn't in on it as she claimed, what other explanation could there be for a photographer knowing exactly where they would go to eat and the exact time? The more Heidi thought about it, she wondered if the whole tyre slashing incident had been made up. Heidi hadn't actually seen the car. For all she knew Craig could have picked it up after they'd left the centre.

She gazed down onto the road from her window seat. The normally busy street now only had a few people milling around outside the take-away shops. Her stomach rumbled, reminding her that she hadn't eaten anything all day. A quick look at her watch and she was shocked to see it was 7pm. She swung her legs onto the floor and went in search of her boots and jacket. Though she couldn't really afford it, dinner would have to be a kebab tonight. She didn't have the energy to be standing in the kitchen all night cooking.

Heidi swung open the front door, and gasped at

the sight of Vanessa.

'What are you doing here?'

'I nearly didn't find this place. I was just about to give up,' Vanessa said with a faint smile. 'I couldn't remember the number—'

'You still haven't answered me.' Heidi wasn't about to be taken in again, no matter how alluring Vanessa appeared.

'Why do you think I'm here?'

Heidi stared hard at her. Wanting her to get the message loud and clear. That Heidi had meant what she had said in Vanessa's office. Every last word.

'I'm not a mind reader, Vanessa. Just say whatever you've got to say. I'm on my way out.'

Vanessa raised her eyebrows. 'On a date?'

'No, to get food. I haven't eaten today; I've had too much on my mind.'

'Me?'

'Don't flatter yourself,' Heidi said as she stepped onto the landing outside and pulled the door shut behind her.

Vanessa sighed. 'I take it you're still pissed off with me?'

'Are you always so observant?'

'We can't carry on like this. Let's go somewhere where we can talk. I saw an Indian restaurant across the road.'

Indian? Kebab? Indian? Kebab? Heidi debated with her stomach. *Vanessa and Indian? Or kebab and TV? Mmm.* Her stomach won. 'All right.'

'Great! Then we can come back up for a drink?' Vanessa asked hopefully as they walked along the balcony.

Heidi's heart screamed yes but her mind was firmly in the no camp. Seeing how much trouble her heart had caused her last time, she decided to go with the latter. 'No. I think it's safer being in public with you. No more meetings behind closed doors.'

Vanessa's triumphant smile faded all the way to nothing. 'Never?'

'Never.'

Vanessa shrugged nonchalantly. 'Suit yourself. Dinner it is then.'

Heidi trailed behind Vanessa as she walked downstairs and across to the restaurant where they were greeted warmly by Ali the owner. Heidi had only eaten there a couple of times when Amanda had treated her, so she was surprised that he remembered her.

'Ah, good to see you again. Come,' Ali said guiding them to a secluded table at the back of the packed restaurant. 'Sanjay, bring the menus.'

The restaurant hummed with conversation as they sat opposite each other inspecting their menus. The soft glow of candlelight made for a romantic setting, which was the last thing Heidi needed.

This was a bad idea. A very bad idea.

The heat rose to Heidi's face when Vanessa's knee brushed against hers. She craned her neck to look for Sanjay. When she turned back Vanessa was staring at her with a grin on her face.

'You looking for someone?' Vanessa asked.

Where's Sanjay with my beer? I need a beer. 'No. Should I be?'

'Not if Craig has any sense,' Vanessa said awkwardly. 'I spoke to him about us being followed.'

'So he admitted it?'

'Yes.'

'And you're still claiming you knew nothing about it?' *Stop looking into her eyes.*

'I know you don't know me very well, but that's not how I get the things I want.'

'No? So what's your way?'

'I think you know that already.'

Vanessa's knee touched Heidi's only this time it stayed pressed against hers. *Oh, God help me!*

'Beer.' Sanjay stopped by their table and placed a beer each in front of them. 'You ready to order?'

This time Heidi felt compelled to look at Vanessa and when Vanessa stared back at her, the longing in her eyes was plain to see. Heidi was grateful they were in a public place. If they had been in her apartment she would have let Vanessa do whatever she wanted to her, regardless of the consequences.

'Um, I'll have the chicken korma and mushroom fried rice please,' Heidi said. She felt conspicuous, as if Sanjay could read the filthy thoughts stampeding through her mind, so she kept her eyes lowered when he took her menu.

'The same please,' Vanessa said.

Sanjay grinned and retreated from the table.

'You look hot,' Vanessa said.

Heidi could tell her statement was meant to be ambiguous by her sheepish grin.

'Do I?' Heidi took a mouthful of beer before resting the ice-cold bottle against her burning cheek.

'The same look you had yesterday.'

A bolt of adrenaline shot through Heidi's body. She shifted uncomfortably as Vanessa leant over and whispered so only Heidi could hear her. 'In fact, if I remember clearly, you were so hot we—'

'All right, you've made your point,' Heidi said, melting at the memory.

Vanessa's eyebrows furrowed, her expression unsure. 'Don't tell me you regret it.'

'Not regret, no.' Heidi tried to ignore the throbbing sensation down below. She couldn't help herself, she wanted another one of those electrifying kisses. 'But ....'

Vanessa raised her eyebrows. 'But?'

'I don't know if this is worth it.'

'This? As in?'

Heidi exhaled forcibly. 'Look, I'm not going to deny the effect you have on me—'

'I'm glad to hear it.'

'But that doesn't mean it's right. Your company is going to be responsible for putting my charity out of business.'

'I told you—'

'I don't want to move somewhere else, Vanessa. Renting anywhere in London is going to be extortionate, we have a good deal where we are—'

'I understand—'

'That's just it, you don't. You can't. Even if it's indirect, you're still profiting from our demise, and I don't feel comfortable with that.' Heidi shifted along the seat, out of the booth. 'I can't see you again, Vanessa. I've got to fight for what's right, and I can't do that if I have feelings for you.'

'They're not going to go away, Heidi. Believe me, I've tried.'

'Maybe it's because, despite all of your money, you aren't as strong as me.' Emotion broke in her voice. 'Thanks for the beer.'

Vanessa's eyes dimmed, clouded with sadness and disappointment.

As Heidi turned and walked away, she couldn't help but wonder if she was making the biggest mistake of her life. Giving up so easily, without even trying to find another way.

By the time she got back to her apartment, she realised that she had.

***

The next morning, Heidi was back in the conference room, standing in front of the very same colleagues that were ready to have her hung, drawn and quartered before they even heard the truth the day before. Tiredness possessed her. Sleep had been fleeting as her mind was too wired, too caught up with the fear of never seeing Vanessa again. Trying to think of ways she could have worded things without being so final had been pointless. It was too late now. Heidi had taken her stance, and she was just about to do the same again.

'Right, I have one thing to say before I go any further. Until we are forced to close the doors on the centre, I'm still the manager here. Which means I'm in charge. If anyone doubts my loyalty to the centre, I'd like you to leave now.' She paused as she looked at their solemn faces. 'We have an uphill battle and I'd rather not have internal fighting going on at the same time.'

Nobody moved.

'Good. I'm glad that's settled.' She clasped her hands in front of her. 'Now, I have a couple of ideas that might make them rethink about evicting us. If we fail, at least we'll have bought some time to find new premises and … a new manager.'

Audible gasps sounded around the room.

'Are you leaving?' Harry asked.

'Yes, Harry, I am. As soon as this situation has been dealt with I'm handing in my resignation.'

'Is this because of—'

Hot rebellion swept over her. Why shouldn't she say exactly what was on her mind? After years of self-sacrifice spent putting her life and energy into the centre, she had earned the right to be honest about her true feelings.

Wearily she said, 'Let's just say the dreadful way you all ganged up on me yesterday swayed my decision, but it's not the only reason. It's time to move on.

Simone, can I see you in my office?'

Simone's face paled. The once easy familiarity they had shared was gone, replaced with a strained politeness. Heidi didn't know if they would be able to find their way back to how things were.

Simone stood and trailed behind her without saying a word. Once in Heidi's office, Simone closed the door behind her and remained by the door while Heidi stood a few feet away.

'Heidi, before you say a word—'

'If you're going to apologise about your behaviour yesterday, don't bother.'

'The only thing I'm sorry about is calling you out in front of everyone. Nothing else. You were bang out of order going behind our backs with that woman and you know it. The Heidi I know would never put our charity on the line for someone who wants to destroy us.'

'And the Simone I knew would have come to me first, before humiliating me and undermining my authority.'

Simone snorted. 'Authority?'

'Yes, authority. Whether you like it or not, manager is my title not yours. For now, anyway. Yesterday is irrelevant. We need to focus on the future—'

'So she dumped you then?'

'No, she didn't dump me. There wasn't anything going on—'

'Jesus, this is me you're talking to, Heidi. I saw the way you two were looking at each other in those photos and to my eyes, there was a lot going on.'

'In your eyes is exactly right. Look, if you can't move past this I really think—'

'I love this centre and I'm not going to let anyone close it down. So, if you say you're gonna do right by this place I believe you.'

'Good, so let's get started.' Heidi dropped onto her seat and grabbed a pad and pen. 'Right, we're going to campaign against those bastards—hard. We are not going to go down without taking them with us.'

'I like it.'

Heidi tapped the pen against the edge of her desk. 'Not through the press. This time we're going to go directly to the people through social media. As well as any businesses that are associated with Berkley O'Neil. We need to find other victims who have been stiffed by them.'

Heidi's tough streak was a trait that had always lain dormant under her compassion, waiting for the right circumstances. That time was now.

Chapter Twenty-Two

Kelli knew Vanessa and Craig thought she was blind to what went on in the family business but they couldn't have been more wrong. She knew exactly what they were up to—well, Craig anyway. Numbers were Kelli's thing. She'd always had a knack for understanding complex calculations, the same way in which hackers knew how to bypass security systems. After stumbling across the financial papers in Vanessa's office, she knew something fishy was going on in the company. Kelli liked to think of herself as a spy working for MI5 and, in this instance, she wanted to find out how deep down the rabbit hole the corruption went. This was why she was crouching behind a car parked across the street from Craig's house, waiting for him to leave for work. He worked from home a lot and she didn't doubt he kept private files in his office. Gaining access to his house would be easy; Kelli still had a key, the one she'd forgotten to give back when she'd stayed there a few nights after her mum died.

Kelli shifted from foot to foot in an attempt to quell the butterflies in her stomach. *Maybe this is a mistake.* She had to find evidence of his wrongdoings for her plan to succeed. *Stop being a baby and just do it.*

It wasn't long before the large oak door opened and Craig breezed towards his black Bentley parked on his drive. He gave himself a once over in the window's reflection and, despite his bulk, gracefully slipped into the car. Seconds later, he drove off, his lack of signalling causing the drivers behind him to hoot their horns in anger. Craig ignored them as usual.

Kelli waited a few minutes, just to be sure he wasn't coming back. When she was satisfied he'd gone for the day she crossed the road, her eyes scanning the immediate vicinity. If he caught her entering his house, there'd be hell to pay—for Kelli and Vanessa, who Craig would no doubt blame for Kelli's wayward actions. Despite her trembling hands, it took less than a minute for her to get inside the property.

Craig didn't have any kids, so his house was immaculate, not a thing out of place.

As Kelli crept along the polished wooden floor, she kept her ears open for any unfamiliar sounds. Craig hired prostitutes on a regular basis, so Kelli had to be careful in case one of the women were still in the house.

Kelli quickly made her way towards his office on the ground floor. The room had an overpowering smell of leather and polish. She walked over to his mahogany desk and looked around in the desk drawer for the key to his cabinet. Finding it, she inserted the key into the filing cabinet positioned at the side of his desk and opened the top drawer. It was full of neat, orderly files. She worked from front to back, pulling out random files and giving them a quick scan. To her dismay, there was no smoking gun to be found. She moved to the drawer below, then finally the bottom one. Nothing. Letting out a long sigh, she replaced the files and pushed the drawer, but something stopped it. On her knees, she reached behind and her fingers made contact with a thick folder. Kelli sank back on her haunches and opened it. It took her only a few seconds to realise what she was holding in her hands. *Bingo!*

Kelli couldn't believe her eyes. They were plans for the Young Minds' site, only they were different to the ones she'd looked at in Vanessa's office. Flipping through the papers, she came across a list of financial transactions. One payment stood out: *Oust Enterprises*. Craig had scribbled 'Jason Lee' next to it. *Who's Jason Lee?*

Kelli didn't have time to contemplate it, so she pushed herself to her feet and crossed over to the photocopier. It took her a few minutes to photocopy everything she needed and to replace the papers in order.

Kelli didn't feel guilty for making copies. She wasn't the one in the wrong, Craig was. A noise from upstairs made her freeze. Footsteps. *Shit, there's someone else in the house.* With the stealth of a thief, she quickly replaced all the papers as neatly as she could in the folder, shoved it at the back of the drawer and closed it. The footsteps stopped. *Move! Move!*

Putting the key back in the drawer, Kelli grabbed the evidence, stuffed it inside her jacket and dashed for the front door. She was outside within seconds, closing the door quietly behind her. Her thoughts were no longer concerned with who was in the house.

She had an urgent delivery to make.

Chapter Twenty-Three

Monday would be a day that Heidi, and Berkley O'Neil for that matter, would never forget. She had spent the weekend ironing 'Save Young Minds' stickers onto white t-shirts. A large part of her didn't want to go down the route she had chosen, but Craig had left her no choice. She wasn't going to be bullied and threatened by a misogynistic jerk. Why couldn't he have left Vanessa to deal with things? They would have easily come to some sort of agreement that suited both parties. But no, he had to stick his oar in, no doubt because Heidi had turned down his advances and had not faded beneath him like a wilted flower. In truth, she couldn't wait until it was all over. When they finally knew their fate. Good or bad.

Relations had returned to normal at the centre. This was due to Heidi holding her hands up and admitting she had handled the situation badly. She acknowledged she shouldn't have seen Vanessa, especially behind her colleagues' backs, but that still didn't change the fact that she was leaving. It was high time someone else took the reins. *Someone without so much personal baggage and debt.*

'Right, listen up.' She clapped her hands to draw her colleagues' attention. 'Christina, I want you to drum up some support from gay businesses in Soho. Cafés, sex shops, I don't care. We need people with banners in support of the centre to line the street outside Berkley O'Neil's offices. If you can't find enough people, then do the rent-a-crowd thing. Offer some of our centre t-shirts or Harry's homemade cakes. Do what you have to do. Just make it happen.'

Christina put her hand to her right temple in salute style. 'I'm on it,' she said with a smile.

Heidi continued to bark out orders as she read down her list on her writing pad. 'We need someone to hand out the t-shirts for the supporters before we start our march.'

'Consider it done,' Richie called out.

'Who wants to be in charge of refreshments?'

Mel raised her hand. 'Me.'

'Handing out leaflets?'

'I will,' Harry said lifting a box from the table.

'Good. That's all we need for now. I'm going to tweet and update Facebook. I'll meet everyone outside at ten.'

Heidi headed for her office and slumped onto her chair. Her body was limp from exhaustion. The only thing that was keeping her going was coffee and adrenaline. They had worked hard for this day and she was determined for it to mean something. Simone had photocopied the photos of Heidi and Vanessa eating at the Mexican restaurant. She was going to take the sting out of Craig's bite by distributing the photos before he got the chance.

At ten minutes to ten, Heidi stepped outside the centre and blinked away the tears that threatened to fall.

There were at least one hundred people outside the centre. *People do care.* Each of them carried a banner with wording in support of the protest.

'Save Our Centre' and 'Principles First, Money Second', 'Berkley O'Neil are homophobic' was a third one. One even read 'Berkley O'Neil make Queer Decision'.

As Heidi led the crowd along Camden Road, members of the media began to arrive and photographers clicked away.

One of the radio reporters turned on her voice recorder and spoke to Heidi in between her chants.

'Will this protest reach its objective of stopping the centre from being closed down?' asked the reporter.

'I'm willing to chain myself to the building if I have to. The centre has been here for many years, serving the gay teenage community of London and cannot be removed just because filthy rich business people want to become even richer.'

A print journalist chatted to another protester who was walking beside Heidi holding a large vibrator. 'The rich cannot discriminate against those with different sexual preferences,' the female protester said. 'This is 2017 and we live in a democratic country. We won't be screwed.'

By the time Heidi and the protesters arrived at the front of the Berkley O'Neil building, the turnout had gained even more protesters along the way. 'Save Young Minds, save Young Minds!' shouted a protestor, whose chant was soon joined in by others. Heidi stood on top of a small side wall and called the protestors to order. Ironically, it was Pricilla Jones who pushed her way to the front to get the best position.

Heidi's voice shook as she looked into the sea of faces in front of her. 'London belongs to all people of any race, colour, creed or sexual preference but Berkley O'Neil don't care. They don't care who they have to tread on to increase the size of their bank balance. But there comes a time when enough is enough. We are here to make a stand. To show them we will not be bullied or blackmailed.'

Heidi saw Simone mingling in the crowd, handing out the photo of Vanessa and herself. This, more than anything, seemed to be what the media was interested in.

Heidi brushed her hair aside. 'Craig O'Neil intended to blackmail me by releasing this photo to the press. An innocent dinner meeting I had with Vanessa O'Neil.' She looked down and caught sight of the picture Priscilla was holding. The memory of that night came flooding back and it took all the strength she had to go on. 'These are the tactics this company uses to shut down the little people, but I say it's time the little people pushed back.'

The crowd clapped and hollered as Heidi jumped off the wall and was immediately grabbed by Priscilla. It took another hour before Heidi was done with all of the interviews. The protestors were enjoying the media coverage and chanted in the background as the television news cameras kept rolling. To no one's surprise the police were soon on the scene moving them on, but it didn't matter, they had achieved what they set out to do. Now they just had to wait for Berkley O'Neil's response. Heidi's gut feeling said they wouldn't respond and, as the hours ticked by, she was proven right. There wasn't a single peep from Vanessa or Craig.

Just before Heidi was going to call it a day, she heard a familiar voice. Within seconds, Amanda appeared at her office doorway making her jump.

'Hey, what are you doing here?'

'Nice reception.' Amanda walked in, gave Heidi a quick hug then dropped her bag on the desk. 'I hope you aren't letting fame go to your head.'

Heidi rolled her eyes. 'Fame? Yeah right.'

'Who would have thought it, my little sister the celebrity.'

'Hardly.'

'Are you kidding? You looked sensational. Who knew you were so photogenic.'

Heidi gave a short laugh. 'Do you think I did the right thing?'

'Do you even have to ask? No one tries to blackmail my sister and gets away with it. I must say though, you and that Vanessa woman looked a cute couple.'

Heidi's stomach turned over as images of Vanessa flashed through her mind. 'Yeah, well, that's dead in the water. I don't think she'll ever want to talk to me again.'

'Whatever's meant to be—'

'Will be.' Heidi finished for her.

A soft sigh escaped Amanda's lips. 'That's right. It will.'

'Amanda.'

'Uh huh?'

'Can I ask you something?' Since Heidi was hell bent on setting the world to rights, it was time to confront Amanda and find out exactly what was going on in her marriage. She hated the thought of her sister not being able to share her burden with anyone.

'Of course,' Amanda said taking a seat.

'Is everything all right between you and Ellis?'

Amanda's eyes narrowed. For a moment, Heidi thought she was going to tell her to mind her own business but just as she was about to retract her question, she saw tears in Amanda's eyes. Heidi jumped out of her seat, made her way around to Amanda and knelt down before her. Taking Amanda's hands in her own, she said, 'What is it? Tell me. If you're worried about mum and dad finding out—'

'It doesn't matter. You're all going to find out sooner or later.'

'Find out what?'

'He left me.'

'What?! No way. Ellis loves you.'

'Not anymore. It's my own stupid fault.'

'Don't blame yourself, Mandy. He should support your decision to work so hard.'

'It's nothing to do with work.' She cast her eyes downwards. A look of shame crossed her features. 'We were … swingers.'

Heidi laughed. 'Of course you were. Come on, be serious.'

Amanda looked up. The expression on her face told Heidi she really was serious.

'Oh,' was all Heidi could think to say. *Amanda, a swinger?* She didn't even want to follow that thought with an image.

'He left me for one of the women we swapped with weeks ago. I didn't even want to do it in the first place, but he kept pushing and pushing so in the end I gave in.'

Heidi found it hard to believe that weedy, introverted Ellis actually had it in him to swing, let alone leave Amanda.

'Oh shit. I'm so sorry.'

Amanda withdrew her hand and rummaged in her bag for a tissue. 'I'll get over it.'

Heidi returned to her desk to give Amanda some space. 'Do you want me to come back to Mum's with you?'

'No, I'm not looking for sympathy. I only came here to tell you,' she stared at her, 'that I'm so proud of you.'

Tears sprung to Heidi's eyes. She had waited twenty-nine years for her big sister to say those words to her.

Chapter Twenty-Four

By the time Vanessa returned to her office, her head was pounding. Spending the morning with Craig had left her dizzy, nauseous and clammy. They had been to Brighton to look at a new property the company was interested in purchasing. Half way through the tour of the site, the call had come through to inform them that a 'mob' had gathered outside their offices.

It was no surprise to her that Heidi had moved things up a gear; she'd been expecting it, but Craig was furious, ranting and raving in her ear for the rest of the morning as well as on the drive back. Now in the sanctuary of her own space, she searched in her drawer for a couple of much needed painkillers.

Knocking the tablets back with a swig of water, Vanessa closed her eyes and rested her forehead on the desk. There was no point in trying to work; she wouldn't be able to concentrate, not when her mind was filled with so much unnecessary drama. *How long is this fight going to go on for*? In a way, she blamed herself. *I should never have got involved. I should have left Craig to deal with Heidi from the start.* Either way, Vanessa concluded, her reputation was going to be tarnished. *Birds of a feather flock together.*

She wasn't wholly convinced that Heidi's vendetta against their company was purely about the eviction alone. It may have been at the start, but not anymore.

She believed what drove Heidi now was her need to get one over on, not only Craig, but Vanessa herself, that the need to punish Vanessa was blurring her vision.

Vanessa should have learnt throughout her years in the business world to never mix business with pleasure—no matter how tempting.

A knock on the door preceded Craig's new secretary hovering in the doorway, looking as stressed as Vanessa felt.

'Ms O'Neil.'

Vanessa reluctantly lifted her head and looked up. 'Call me Vanessa.'

'Okay sorry. Um, Craig wants to see you in his office.'

The thought of spending another second in Craig's company made Vanessa feel uneasy. 'Suzy, can you tell him I'm busy, please. I'll—'

'He said it's urgent,' Suzy's voice quivered.

Vanessa noticed Suzy's red puffy eyes. Craig had obviously scared the living daylights out of her with his tantrums and demands. There was no need for her to make Suzy's day any worse, so Vanessa pushed back her chair and stood.

'Why don't you go and get yourself a coffee. I'll deal with Craig.'

Suzy shot her a grateful smile. 'Thank you.'

Vanessa walked down the corridor, dreading to think what had pissed Craig off now, not that it took much these days.

'So what's the urgency?' she said, trying to look

interested as she entered Craig's office.

Craig stood in front of the TV leering at the screen, his pupils practically glowing red with hatred.

'That bitch has gone too far,' Craig almost shrieked. 'She's been badmouthing me, sprouting shit about me blackmailing her!'

Vanessa looked at him bemused. 'But you did, didn't you?'

He spun around and glared at her. 'Whose fucking side are you on? You do realise this affects you as much as it does me.'

'I'm well aware of that Craig, but don't say I didn't warn you.'

The news footage panned across the crowds and zoomed in on Heidi. Vanessa drew in a sharp breath when her face filled the screen. Instead of sharing the rage Craig exuded, Vanessa felt strangely moved by Heidi and the support she had garnered for her cause. Vanessa knew if the circumstances were different, she too would be out there with the crowd trying to save the centre. Instead, she was one of the bad guys indirectly responsible for the closure. It was a cross she would just have to bear.

'Did you hear that?! We're corrupt? Some insignificant little bitch has an opinion about us, but she doesn't stop there, oh no!' Craig raged, his face crimson as he clutched his Scotch. 'She's plastered our name all over a fuck load of social media pages, consumer watchdogs and has contacted our associates!'

'She what?' Vanessa unsteadily lowered herself

onto the sofa and stared at the screen. Heidi was speaking to several journalists in front of the centre. *This is bad.* It was one thing to have a protest outside the building, but to contact their business associates? She had to agree with Craig—that was going a step too far.

Does she hate me this much that she would smear the reputation of my father's company? Vanessa couldn't believe that the woman she'd almost made love to a few nights before wanted to destroy them by spreading lies. The company was nothing like the one she was portraying.

'She has to be stopped,' Vanessa said.

'This is what I've been telling you, but your head has been stuck in the clouds. She is not who you think she is.' Craig slammed his glass down on the desk and grabbed his jacket, pulling it on as he headed for the door.

'Where are you going?'

'To see our solicitor. I'm going to find out where we stand with her making slanderous accusations. I'll make sure I take that bitch down! I want her out of the way, out of that building and fucking gone, once and for all!'

Vanessa relaxed once he'd stormed out without another word. She didn't need Craig to tell her they had to act, but what if, and it was a big if, Heidi was right? That there was some truth to her claim that the company was corrupt? Craig's underhandedness was, after all, the reason Vanessa had elected to come into the fold after so many years of resisting. She knew Craig was very capable of destroying their company with his unorthodox and sometimes unethical business conduct, but did Heidi have any evidence of her claims?

Losing herself in Heidi's eyes took her back to the night in her apartment. Vanessa could still remember the smell of her hair and the slight hint of her perfume just above her collarbone. Vanessa's gaze dropped to Heidi's lips and remembered them hard pressed against her own.

Behind Heidi, one slogan in the crowd caught her eye in particular. Not because it was so harsh—*Down with the O'Neil bullies*—no, what shocked her to her core was the face beneath the banner.

'Kelli?' she breathed out her name. 'What the hell is she doing there?'

Vanessa couldn't believe her eyes. The camera panned and stopped on Heidi again.

'You have to understand we're not a business, we're a charity, and that means we care about people, not money. Our centre serves society on behalf of young people who can't manage by themselves. Where will you go if you feel as if the world is against you? Young people who feel suicidal, who are alone in an intolerant world, they find peace with us. And why? Because most of us have been there. People need the centre. Berkley O'Neil does not.'

'You're watching it too?' Suzy remarked from the doorway. She walked to Craig's desk and laid several papers down. 'What do you really think she's after?'

'Justice,' Vanessa replied, too dazed to consider anything other than Kelli and what her appearance at the protest meant.

'I didn't want to raise the issue while Craig was here,' Suzy said, 'but my sister sent my nephew to the centre because he was having a hard time coming to terms with his sexuality. The counselling he received there was second to none; I dread to think what would have happened if he'd had nowhere to turn.'

'I'm glad things worked out for him,' Vanessa said. 'The place sounds like a sanctuary.'

'It is,' Suzy said before leaving Vanessa to her thoughts.

Heidi had disappeared from the screen, but the crowd was still on camera. Vanessa leant forward, searching for Kelli again. *My niece. My off-kilter, lost and angry niece.* Vanessa just couldn't make sense of it. *Why would she oppose our company, a company she holds shares in?*

It was mind boggling. *Unless she's gay. But why wouldn't she tell me, it's not as if she has to be scared of rejection?* It had never crossed her mind to ask Kelli about dating. This past year Vanessa was frightened to ask her about anything to do with her life, worried about the backlash it would cause; and now this. If the press realised who Kelli was, it would crush them, to have someone within their own family opposing a business decision.

It didn't take Vanessa long to realise that it was probably what Kelli wanted all along.

Chapter Twenty-Five

Despite the protest being a success in bringing more attention to the centre's cause, the eviction date still loomed depressingly close. In three weeks, it would all be over; that was unless a miracle happened. Heidi wasn't going to hold her breath. Although she went through the motions of cheering on the efforts of her colleagues, personally Heidi had given up. There had been no contact from Vanessa or Craig and it was now obvious the negative reports about them failed to have any effect. Worse of all, because of Heidi's unrealistic vendetta to try and bring them down, she had lost the one opportunity she may have had to be with Vanessa.

It hadn't been long since that day in the restaurant, but Vanessa still haunted her. Thoughts of her touch, the tenderness of her voice, her eyes and her smile all consumed her. Whenever Heidi's mind drifted, it drifted to her.

A scream brought her attention back to the present, then another. Heidi ran into the corridor; her body alert, ready for action. Simone was running towards her, panting, breathless. Heidi couldn't imagine what had happened. Expecting to see a look of panic on Simone's face as she neared, Heidi frowned when Simone laughed.

'Oh my God, Heidi! You're not going to effing believe this,' Simone said, her eyes were so wide Heidi thought they might pop out.

'Simone, you're scaring me!' Heidi said, thinking the stress had become too much and Simone had lost the plot.

'We just received an anonymous delivery.' Simone handed her an A4-sized envelope. On the front, the words, 'This will help you sink the O'Neils' was scribbled in large clumsy handwriting. 'Mel found it at reception when she got back from a fag break.'

Heidi took the package from her and tore it open like a cat ripping a bag of Dreamies treats. Her frown turned to a beaming smile as she scanned page after page.

'Are you thinking what I'm thinking?' Simone said.

Heidi looked heavenwards. *Thank you, thank you, thank you!* 'You bet I am. We need to read through this carefully.'

'What are we waiting for? I'm right behind you.'

An hour later, Simone and Heidi sat in silence, their mouths agape. From what they understood, Berkley O'Neil had made a contribution to the local authority under section 106 of the Planning Act and in return, the authority waived the company's responsibility to build affordable housing, as well as a community centre.

'The lying scheming conniving bastards,' Simone said as she continued to read from the papers. 'Over the last ten years, Berkley O'Neil hasn't once had to comply with local authority rules on the percentage of new buildings that have to be built with affordable housing.'

'Meaning?' Heidi asked.

'Meaning, the local authority let them off every time. I know that under section 106 they're given some leeway if they make a contribution, but come on! Every time!?'

Heidi scrutinised the papers closer and found that the O'Neils and their associates, Berkley Trust, had bribed planning committee members, in particular one Jason Lee, to approve their planning applications.

'How on earth have they got away with this?' Heidi asked.

'Who's going to question them?' Simone said. 'If the planning committees are in on it.'

'But you'd think someone in the local community would have complained or something?'

'I know it's a long shot, but what if they were paid off too?'

'Or just turned a blind eye because they didn't give a shit?'

'Turncoats, the lot of them.'

'Well this lady is not for turning! If I didn't believe in God before, I sure as hell do now.' Heidi could feel something burning inside her veins. Something she hadn't felt in a long time. Hope. 'Simone, we're going to name and shame those bastards. They'll be sorry they ever bought this building.'

'You almost sound happy to give the O'Neils what they deserve.'

'This isn't about revenge. This is about shining a light on a company that has managed to hide in the dark for way too long.' Heidi clasped her hands in front of her. 'I'm going to—'

'I want to do it. I'll release the papers simultaneously on social media first thing tomorrow. Mel still has the list she compiled of the companies they work with.'

'Okay. Hopefully when word gets out, the mainstream media will pick it up.'

Heidi couldn't help but think how devastating it was going to be for Berkley O'Neil to be exposed by those they'd sought to destroy. If this plan worked, not only would they get to keep the centre, but they'd also topple Berkley O'Neil, crumbling them to the ground.

However, it wasn't that easy. In truth, Heidi felt bad about what they were going to do, especially if it affected Vanessa. She closed her eyes and saw her. For a moment, Heidi could almost feel her breath against her skin, feel her hand caressing ....

'Are you still with me?' Simone asked.

'What? Yes, sorry I was thinking.'

'About?'

Heidi wasn't about to lie to Simone again. Not after last time. 'Vanessa.'

'I thought so.'

'I'm sorry.'

'You really like her, don't you?'

Heidi nodded.

'So, what are you going to do?'

'I don't have a choice do I?'

'You know there'll be no coming back from this once it's been made public.'

'I know, but the truth needs to be told,' Heidi said. 'If we don't expose them now, how many other lives are they going to destroy?'

I'm never going to see her again.

Chapter Twenty-Six

Kelli stumbled to the bathroom, nauseous and weary; her head pounded and the world around her spun. Her first instinct had been to throw up on the floor beside her bed, but somehow, she had managed to get to the toilet under her own steam, a feat that had been a miracle in itself. Once there, she yanked the toilet seat up with one hand and held her hair back with the other. Her stomach heaved and Kelli puked up all the alcohol she had consumed the night before. Having flushed the toilet three times, it did nothing to rid the smell of stale beer which pervaded the room.

Kelli needed to get out of the bathroom as soon as possible. That, however, would have required being able to stand up. She barely had any energy to lift her head. Even though her stomach was completely empty, like a deep pit without a bottom, she couldn't be sure whether she would vomit again if she moved.

Kelli realised she needed water, as she had heard that hangovers were caused by dehydration. With every bit of strength she could muster, she pushed herself to her feet, using the toilet to aid her. Tentatively walking to the door, she opened it and stuck her head out, listening for Maggie. Silence. She put a hand against the wall to guide her along the hallway and down the stairs. Tears sprung to her eyes when she entered the kitchen and remembered the argument that had taken place with

Vanessa. Kelli couldn't understand why she wanted to hurt Vanessa so much, only that she did, more than anything. It was as if by hurting Vanessa, it would somehow lessen her own pain.

Kelli grabbed a bottle of water out of the fridge and a banana from the fruit bowl and took them back upstairs with her. As soon as she reached her bedroom, her mobile phone started ringing. Her intention was to ignore it until it occurred to her it might be Christina.

To her delight, it was her.

'Hey, what you up to?' Christina said. Her voice seemed louder than usual, so Kelli moved the phone away from her ear.

'Nothing much.' Just talking caused her brain to hurt.

'Do you want to come and hang out at mine?'

'Umm.'

'It's not a trick question, Kelli. Yes or no?'

'I ... yeah okay, but I'm going to need a couple of hours.'

'There's no need to get all dressed up for me,' Christina teased.

'As if,' Kelli replied. She needed to find painkillers and have a long soak in the bath. It normally only took an hour to make herself feel better after a drinking session, but last night was no ordinary session. She'd consumed more cans of beer than she ever had before.

'Meet me at Seven Sisters tube station at twelve.' Christina paused. 'Kelli?'

'Uh huh?' Kelli's mind had shifted onto what she

was going to wear.

'I wanted to thank you.'

Jeans and a hoody? 'For what?'

'You know what you did.'

No, it will make me look like a roughneck. 'I don't know what you're on about.'

'The envelope.'

Her heart accelerated. 'What envelope?'

'The one you dropped off at the centre.'

'I—'

'Please don't lie to me. I hate liars.'

'I'll see you at the station at twelve.'

As if on cue, by ten-thirty Kelli's hangover was slowly abating, and she was looking forward to hanging out with Christina. She bounded down the stairs two at a time and headed for the front door. Just as she reached for the handle, Maggie's voice sounded from behind.

'Was that you I heard in the bathroom earlier?'

Kelli leant her forehead against the door. 'Me? Nope.'

'Have you got a minute?'

Kelli gritted her teeth, irritated already by having to answer to Vanessa's spy. 'Not really.'

'I wasn't asking. Here now.' Maggie's voice was firm, telling Kelli she had no choice but to obey.

Kelli exhaled a pent-up breath as she turned and walked towards her.

'I heard you two arguing last night.'

Kelli rolled her eyes. 'Like that's anything new?'

'Why are you so angry with her, Kelli?' Maggie

reached out to her and tried to take hold of her hand. 'What has she done to you?'

Kellie snatched her hands back and put them behind her back, out of reach. She was aware that her complaint was a repetitive one, but it was the one that hurt her the most.

'What hasn't she done, you mean. Let's see. She's meant to be looking after me, but all she does is work—'

'It's not entirely her fault though, is it?'

Kelli gave a bitter laugh. 'It's no surprise you're siding with her. In your eyes, she can do no wrong. She's always been your favourite, hasn't she? You even loved her more than my mum.'

'Don't you talk about things you know nothing about, young lady.'

'Well it's true, isn't it? Why does everyone in this family have to lie about everything?'

Maggie's eyes watered. 'I loved Lauren like she was my own child. It breaks my heart every day that she's not here, but that doesn't mean I have to take my anger out on everyone else.'

'You wouldn't, because you believe in God, don't you? That there's an afterlife where we'll all meet up again and live happily ever after. Well guess what, I'm not a kid anymore. I don't believe in fairy tales.' Kelli narrowed her eyes to stop Maggie from seeing her own pain. 'And at your age, neither should you!'

Kelli turned and stormed out of the house before she broke down in tears and asked Maggie to hold her.

Arriving at the station an hour later, Kelli emerged

from the exit to find Christina waiting for her. They engaged in small talk about Kelli's journey as they walked along the main road, but it wasn't long before the conversation turned to her. Kelli tried not to show how nervous she was. After her encounter with Maggie, the last thing Kelli wanted to do was talk about herself and so started to regret her decision to go to Christina's home.

As they walked side by side along a crescent road, Kelli suddenly felt incredibly self-aware. Even though no one was staring at them, it was as though someone was, as if they could somehow tell that they were gay.

'I didn't tell you who I was related to because I didn't want you to judge me,' Kelli finally said in response to Christina's question.

'You can't think that much of me if you think I'm that shallow.'

Kelli slowed her pace. 'No, never. I'm sorry it came out like that. It's just that—'

Christina's face softened as she glanced at her. 'It's okay, you don't have to explain, I can imagine the shit you must get being related to the O'Neils; they're not exactly beacons of light in the community.'

'They're not that bad. Not really. Well my aunt isn't anyway.' Kelli couldn't believe she had just stuck up for Vanessa. It was one thing for Kelli to slag her off but she wouldn't tolerate it from anyone else. 'It's Craig who's the nasty one.'

'I live here,' Christina said, gesturing to a large Victorian house.

'Alone?' Kelli brought her right hand up to her breastbone. *She's not going to jump your bones you idiot.*

'Nah, a house share.'

The tension in Kelli's shoulders receded. 'Oh.'

'Don't worry, no one's home. They'll all be at university.'

Kelli followed her inside the house, closing the door behind her. The interior had a strange antiseptic smell about it. She walked around a pile of mail that had been ignored and pushed against a wall. The carpet in the hallway looked like it hadn't been hoovered in some time. Crumbs and footprints were interspersed here and there at various intervals.

'I'll get us a drink,' Christina said, indicating for Kelli to go into a room at the end of the hallway.

In the living room, several pairs of dirty socks sat on the floor underneath a glass coffee table. Various books lay on the sofa, each with a bookmark sticking out from its pages. Some books were in better condition than others.

A photo of Christina and a group of people, who Kelli assumed to be her house mates, was propped up on the TV. In the picture, they all looked happy and content; leaving Kelli to wonder what it was like to have a network of friends like that. People you could share your dreams, hopes and fears with. *I wonder if they're gay.*

Kelli slumped down on the sofa, moving some of the books to the coffee table to make room. She looked up when Christina returned with a large, full glass of orange juice and handed it to her.

'Thanks,' Kelli said and took a mouthful. It had a tangy, pulpy taste that made her squirm.

Christina laughed at her reaction. 'Sorry it's the cheap stuff. I bet you're used to drinking it freshly squeezed.'

'My aunt's the one into juicing. Give me a coke any day,' Kelli said with a nervous laugh.

Christina sank down onto a chair next to the sofa. She studied Kelli's face for several moments, not saying anything. Kelli looked away. Her pulse raced under Christina's gaze. She was fast regretting her impulsive need to be alone with Christina; now that she was there, all she wanted to do was flee.

At last, Christina broke the silence between them. 'What are you afraid of?'

Kelli took a gulp of orange juice, just so she would have something to do. Her voice shook slightly as she spoke. 'Me?' *You.* 'Nothing.'

'Could have fooled me.' Christina slid over onto the sofa, took Kelli's glass and put it on the table. 'So, what do you want to do?'

Kiss you. Kelli shrugged as she inched away from her.

'I think you do,' Christina said as she extended her hand out towards Kelli.

Kelli saw it moving in slow motion. She bit her bottom lip. A raw, intense, arctic shock ran through her body. She almost let out a cry of surprise. Her mouth, like the rest of her body, was frozen. Her heart was the only part of her that gave any kind of visible movement.

It beat so hard against her chest that she thought her rib cage would break open and splinter through her skin.

Then, as if she had read Kelli's mind, Christina leant in and kissed her.

***

The sheets were rumpled. Clothes were strewn over the floor. Kelli lay naked on the bed, Christina close beside her, stroking Kelli's hair away from her perspiring face. Kelli's body felt as if someone had given her a jolt of electricity. Her muscles were still contracting from the mind-blowing intensity of her first ever orgasm.

'Are you happy?' Christina whispered.

'Do I look happy?' Kelli couldn't wipe away the grin that was plastered on her face.

'Very.'

'Are you?'

Christina scrunched her nose. 'Actually, I think happy is an understatement.'

Then her mouth was on Kelli's again, still as hard and eager as it had been only minutes before.

Kelli wrapped her arms around Christina's back, squeezing her tight. She desperately wanted their bodies to merge into one, so they would never be apart.

'I could kiss you all day,' Christina said pulling away to catch her breath.

'I'd like that.'

'And I will.'

'Forever?'

'Forever.'

Kelli would store this memory in her heart until the day she died. The day she had finally come into her own. She felt liberated. There was no need to fantasise about what could be anymore, or how a woman's touch would feel.

Forever. She loved the sound of that.

'I still can't believe I met you,' Kelli said, rolling on her back and staring up at the ceiling.

'I can. I've always believed everyone has a soulmate.'

Kelli turned her head to face Christina. 'So I'm your soulmate?'

'Yep.'

'Then you must be mine.' Kelli leant over and buried her face in the crook of Christina's neck to hide the tears that brimmed in her eyes. It was times like this that she really missed her mum; moments of life-changing events. She knew if her mum was still alive, they would have spent hours chatting and eating ice cream on the sofa, the way they had throughout her life. Her mum would have loved Christina the same way that she did.

Christina's arms cradled her, rocking her gently as she kissed her. 'Shhh,' she comforted. 'It's okay to cry. Your mum knows you're happy now.'

Kelli drew back; tears blurred her vision. 'How … how did you know?'

'You don't hide your pain very well. Besides, I don't think anyone ever gets over the death of a parent. Not really. I can't imagine how hard it must be for you.'

'I'm sorry; I didn't mean to spoil things.'

'Hey, are you crazy. This is what being in a relationship is about. It's not all about sex. With me it isn't anyway. We lean on each other, lend a hand when the other is down.'

'Not in my family. They just ignore you in the hope that you'll go away.'

'Are you talking about your aunt?'

Kelli nodded.

'I'm not taking sides, but people grieve in their own way. Your mum was her sister. It must have been tough on her as well. I bet she doesn't talk about it because she feels guilty.'

'Apart from having a lodger she hates, her life hasn't changed much. What has she got to feel guilty about?'

'That she couldn't save her sister; that she somehow let her down when she needed her most.'

'I doubt it. She doesn't care about anyone but herself. It's not going to matter soon anyway. When I'm eighteen, I'll be long gone. Then she can go back to her miserable empty life.'

'Have you actually tried talking to her?'

'There's no point. She wouldn't listen anyway.'

'How do you know if you won't try?'

'Because I know her. If it isn't about work, she isn't interested.'

'You'd be surprised, Kelli. Will you do it for me? Just this once?'

Kelli didn't want to look like a spoilt brat so

relented. Whether she actually went through with it remained to be seen. How could she even start a conversation without Vanessa making an excuse to go back to work? 'Okay, I'll give it a go, but only if ….' She traced the outline of Christina's collar bone.

'Go on.'

'You teach me how to ….' Kelli pressed her face against her ear and whispered the rest.

Christina giggled. 'It would be a pleasure.'

Kelli rolled onto her back and closed her eyes. This was her new life now and she wasn't going to let her happiness be governed by her past; whether it was grief or Vanessa.

Chapter Twenty-Seven

During the drive home, a myriad of contemplations, reasoning, planning and concerns simultaneously ran through Vanessa's mind, but one thought stood out above the others: Kelli's involvement with the centre. They would have to talk about it and she didn't give a damn what kind of mood Kelli was in. Kelli was in her house, under her care and for once, she would not be walking on eggshells for the sake of harmony or because she hated the idea of confronting her niece. Vanessa needed to know what was going on inside her head.

Maggie had left her a pot of chicken soup on the hob and freshly baked rolls on the kitchen counter, under the cover of a red dishcloth. The aroma filled the whole house, reminding Vanessa of her childhood. That feeling of safety, the shelter of innocence and the freedom of no priorities or responsibilities permeated through her as she spooned out a bowl of soup.

The home-cooked meal was a welcome change to the take-aways she'd been indulging in during the past week. Vanessa sat down at the island and switched on the small TV. She chose a channel with a nature documentary that featured Richard Attenborough's soothing narration, because she'd learnt one thing over the years: an active, but calm home, automatically made for a more relaxed conversation, even if the conversation involved her prying into Kelli's secrets.

The front door slammed. Footsteps made their way towards the kitchen, then stopped abruptly and turned in the other direction. Vanessa was off her seat in seconds and at the door.

'Hey.'

Kelli turned. Dread in her eyes.

'Don't play all shy now. I thought you'd be proud of yourself after your TV appearance.'

'So you saw me on TV and what?' Kelli said.

'And what?' Vanessa sensed Kelli's defences rise up around her. *This is going to be fun,* Vanessa mused, getting mentally ready for a feisty tug-of-war. 'What were you doing at the centre?'

'I don't have to answer that. I don't owe you anything. Once I'm eighteen I'll be getting out of this hell hole.'

Vanessa was dumbfounded. 'Hell hole?'

'Yes, hell hole,' Kelli spat. 'You and Craig are an embarrassment. Do you know how it feels to have people gossiping about your family behind your back? Even people at college pass remarks about the heartless O'Neil empire and paint me with the same brush.'

Vanessa remained silent. In truth, she didn't know how to respond to that point. Kelli was right, which made it hard to argue with.

'So that's why you were protesting with them. Because you think I'm heartless?'

Doubt clouded Kelli's eyes. 'If you aren't, how can you go along with the closure? What makes it even worse is that you're gay. I thought minorities stuck together.'

'In an ideal world, they would, but we run a business, not a charity.' Vanessa knew it was a cop out, even as she said it. 'So, tell me, what's your interest in the centre?'

Visibly flustered, Kelli ran her fingers through her hair but said nothing.

'Are you going to tell me?'

Kelli refused to answer or look Vanessa in the eye. Shifting uncomfortably, her eyes combed the floor.

'I asked you a question.' Vanessa wasn't relenting. 'I know what kind of services they offer there. Are you gay? You can tell me.'

Kelli's eyes widened to Vanessa's candid prying; her bottom lip trembled before she gripped it between her teeth.

'Yes, I'm gay! Are you happy now? Your niece is a dyke just like you! Now you can get your Public Relations team to put it out in a media statement so that the whole world can know!'

Vanessa ignored her outburst. 'Is this what's been troubling you all this time? Because if it is, you can talk to me you know,' she said casually, although her heart was thundering in her chest, praying Kelli would open up to her.

Slowly, Kelli raised her eyes. 'Yes.'

Breakthrough! Vanessa was so overwhelmed, that she could have thrust her fist in the air in triumph. She tried not to look pleased, knowing Kelli would construe it as ridicule or smugness.

Vanessa walked up to Kelli and placed her hands

on her shoulders. 'I'm glad that you feel comfortable enough to share this with me. I can only imagine how hard it's been for you recently. Not just about your sexuality, but everything.'

Kelli studied her face. Vanessa wanted to pull her into her arms and hug the life out of her. Kelli was coming back to her.

'Why didn't you tell me?' Vanessa asked as she dropped her arms to her side and stepped back to give Kelli some space.

Kelli shrugged. 'I thought you wouldn't believe me. That I was having an identity crisis.'

'Jesus, Kelli, is that what you really thought? That I wouldn't believe the person I love more than anything on this earth?'

Kelli sneered at her. 'If that's true then why are you trying to close down the only place I went to for help when there was no one else?'

'Listen—'

'No, you listen!' Tears brimmed in her eyes. 'All you care about is money! Work and money! That's all that matters to you, so don't pretend you care about me. It's fucking sick what you're doing to all those people who need the centre. You're worse than Craig; at least he doesn't pretend to care. I fucking hate you!'

Kelli made for the door whilst sobbing and Vanessa's heart caved in under the sledgehammer of her attack.

Chapter Twenty-Eight

After a long day at the centre, Heidi arrived home, wanting nothing more than to soak in a hot bath and to have an early night. She didn't even want dinner; she was that tired. The street lamps had blown again, pitching the pathway to her block of flats into darkness. Heidi pulled her phone out of her coat pocket and held her finger ready to speed dial the police should someone lunge out at her from the tall brushes up ahead. Under the full moon, she scanned the area to discern any kind of motion in the communal garden. Visions of Jack the Ripper played on her mind, no matter how much she tried to convince herself that he had died decades ago.

Heidi safely reached the entrance to her flats and looked up the stairwell when she heard footsteps coming down. Instead of walking up, she waited until the person came into view.

'Vanessa?' she said.

Vanessa gave a slight wave.

'Look, if you've come about—'

'I'm not here about the centre, I need to ....' Her words vanished as they caught in her throat. 'I didn't know where else—'

'Hey, it's okay. Come on, let's go up to my flat. I'll put the kettle on and make you a coffee,' Heidi said, getting a strong whiff of brandy from Vanessa's breath.

'I think I need one.'

From the way Vanessa's body stooped, it was obvious something heavy was on her mind. What, Heidi couldn't imagine.

They made their way up the two flights of stairs in silence. Once inside Heidi's flat, Vanessa wandered around aimlessly, looking at the wall art while Heidi made two cups of coffee.

'Let's sit outside while it's still mild,' Heidi said.

Vanessa gestured for Heidi to lead the way. Simone had gifted her outdoor lights for the balcony a few weeks ago, which Heidi had skilfully attached along the edge of the wall.

'Wow, it looks lovely out here,' Vanessa said as she dropped onto a chair.

'This is my own little piece of heaven,' Heidi said, lighting three candles on the small wooden table.

Vanessa slid off her jacket and hung it on the back of her chair.

'So, what's the matter?' Heidi asked when she finally sat down.

'Where do you want me to start?' Vanessa cast her a look with her enthralling eyes that left Heidi weak.

'At the beginning normally helps.'

Vanessa bowed her head and ran her hands through her hair. 'I'm a failure.'

'Who? You? Are you kidding me?'

Vanessa let out a long sigh. 'It's true. With the things that matter anyway.'

'Like what? You're beautiful, intelligent and you drive the most amazing car—'

'Yes, but it's all materialistic. I'd give it all up to ….'

'To?' Heidi pressed, anxious to know what was more important than never having to worry about what the future held.

'To connect with my niece.'

'Your niece?' Heidi was not expecting to hear that. 'I'm sorry, but I'm confused. Why are you having problems with her?'

'She's under my care—'

'Really?'

'Until she's eighteen anyway.'

'Where're her parents?'

'My … my sister … died.'

Heidi's hand flew to her mouth. 'Oh God, I'm sorry, Vanessa.'

Vanessa waved her apology away. 'I feel as if I'm letting her slip through my fingers. No matter what I do, or how I approach her, she just locks me out,' she explained; her breath-taking grey eyes looked pristine in the faint glare of the romantic candle light.

'How old is she?'

'Sixteen.'

'Tough age. Do you mind me asking when her mother died?' Heidi caught herself. She didn't want to make things even more emotional for Vanessa. 'Sorry, I shouldn't have asked.'

'It's okay. I'm here because I need to talk to someone. My sister committed suicide.' Her voice broke and tears ran freely down her cheeks. 'Craig bullied her when she was alive. He hated her because he thought she was a failure for falling pregnant at eighteen. He really thinks he's so bloody perfect.'

Heidi nodded, not about to break Vanessa's train of thought.

'I feel like I'm not doing enough to get her out of her shell, to show her how much I care. I was so wrapped up in my own life, travelling the world and having fun while Lauren was teetering on the edge of a chair with a fucking noose around her neck.'

Heidi's chest ached, empathetic to her bare sorrow. She placed her hand over Vanessa's.

'And now I'm abandoning Kelli by throwing myself into my work instead. Some aunt, eh?' Vanessa held her gaze for a moment. 'No wonder Kelli's been going to your centre—'

'Wait, Kelli's your niece? Of course,' Heidi said as she remembered the very attractive girl who had been hanging out with Christina recently. *I thought she looked familiar.* It all made sense where those anonymous files had come from—not that she'd say a word about it to Vanessa.

'Yes,' Vanessa said, looking up at her. 'Do you know her? Have you spoken to her?'

'A few times. She seems to be a well-adjusted young woman. A little reserved, but most teenagers are,' Heidi replied.

'She told me she's gay and that she thought I wouldn't believe her.'

'Why would she think that?'

Vanessa gave Heidi a cursory glance. 'I have no idea. I've been racking my brain to think of an incident that would make her think that, but I just keep coming up blank.'

'Well the fact she told you should tell you something,' Heidi said. 'That must have been a big step for her. It shows she trusts you despite everything else that's going on around you.'

The air between them took on the feeling of a force field, and for a moment, Heidi could do nothing but lose herself in Vanessa's eyes. Her stomach churned when Vanessa reached behind her chair for her jacket and slipped it on.

'I'd better go. I don't even know why I came here.' Vanessa pushed herself onto her feet. 'You've got enough on your plate without me going on about my own problems.'

Heidi stood toe-to-toe with Vanessa. It took every ounce of control not to pull her into her arms. 'I think you should stay the night,' she said, hoping it didn't sound like an opportunistic pick-up line.

Vanessa arched an eyebrow. 'You think so?'

'I do.'

'Where will I sleep?'

'In my bed.'

'With you?' A smile crept onto her lips.

'Unless you want to sleep on the sofa.'

Vanessa's gaze moved from Heidi's face to her chest; the heat in her eyes told Heidi all she needed to know. The voice that had been telling her to stop things before they went any further held less sway than it had before. Yes, shit was going to hit the fan in the morning, but if Vanessa knew what was going to be unleashed, she wouldn't stay a second longer and Heidi didn't want that. She had let Vanessa go before and she wasn't going to do it again, not tonight anyway. They had made a connection and the night was theirs.

Nothing, not the centre, business or Craig was going to stand between them now.

Vanessa shrugged out of her jacket in what Heidi thought was the sexiest move she'd ever seen before. As her jacket fell to the floor, Vanessa peeled off her top, shaking her hair loose out of its ponytail. Heidi strangled a moan, knowing what was coming.

Vanessa eliminated what little space there was between them and kissed her hard. Heidi kissed back; her hands found their way to Vanessa's backside and pulled her close as she wedged her leg between Vanessa's thighs. Vanessa let out a soft sigh as she rubbed against Heidi's leg muscle.

Vanessa wrenched her mouth from Heidi's; struggling for breath she said, 'Inside.'

Heidi didn't have to be told twice. They stumbled into the living room and Vanessa guided Heidi onto the sofa before quickly removing Heidi's jeans and underwear. Vanessa fell to her knees in front of her and Heidi cradled her head, gripping her hair in her fists.

Vanessa's voice was tight with lust when she said, 'I want to taste you.'

Smoothly parting Heidi's legs, Vanessa slid her

hands beneath Heidi's behind forcing her hips upwards, before lowering her mouth until she made contact with the silky centre of Heidi's core.

'Mmm.' A guttural sigh escaped Heidi's lips as she writhed when the tip of Vanessa's tongue made contact.

Vanessa's free hands cupped Heidi's naked breasts, alternating between squeezing and tugging her hard nipples.

Heidi had been touched before, but never like this. Her body was on fire as she opened her eyes and looked down at Vanessa's head between her legs. That in itself was enough to make her come there and then. Vanessa's tongue was a master of control, driving Heidi to the edge as it teased and licked in long sensuous strokes until Heidi thought she was going to explode. As if sensing the end was near for her, Vanessa said, 'Not yet.'

'I have to ….' She pushed Vanessa's mouth harder against her.

Vanessa pulled back. 'If you suffocate me, I won't be able to finish.'

'It's okay,' Heidi whimpered in frustration before forcing her head down again. 'I know CPR.'

Vanessa gave a muffled laugh. She grabbed Heidi behind her neck and brought her mouth to her own. Heidi shuddered as Vanessa's fingers slid between her thighs until she found her swollen nub and then rubbed her wet thumb around it.

'Oh shit,' Heidi said against Vanessa's open mouth as Vanessa's fingers slowly slid deep inside.

'Do you like that?' Vanessa said in a coarse

seductive whisper.

'Fuck, yes … yes,' Heidi panted, bucking and writhing as Vanessa rhythmically thrust into her again and again, picking up speed. Heidi's inner walls tightened around Vanessa's fingers and she cried out, arching her back as each awakened nerve ending quivered. Teetering on the edge of the most powerful orgasm Heidi had ever thought possible, she let out one last cry and finally let go.

Vanessa kept her fingers inside Heidi as her orgasm washed over her. Vanessa's tongue circled Heidi's nipple, her hot mouth then engulfed it. Heidi wanted this moment to last forever. Vanessa was hers for now, and she belonged to Vanessa, even if it was only going to be for one night.

Hours later, they lay on Heidi's bed—naked, spent. Heidi closed her eyes as Vanessa's hand caressed her hair and her warm breath tickled the hairs on the back of her neck. Under beams of moonlight, Heidi lay perfectly still and listened to the heart-wrenching sound of Vanessa crying until some time later, she finally fell asleep.

Chapter Twenty-Nine

The tweeting birds stirred Heidi from her sex-filled dream and it took several seconds for her to realise that last night wasn't a dream after all, that the hot sex had actually happened. She only had to look at the hand covering her breast and feel the warmth from Vanessa's breath on her neck to realise it was a reality. Heidi wanted to laugh, jump out of bed and dance, but refrained to keep from waking Vanessa up. Instead, Heidi carefully slipped Vanessa's hand off her breast and slid out from under her. She was dying to use the toilet, so she made quick work of her reluctant escape.

'Where are you going?' Vanessa asked as Heidi headed toward the bedroom door on tip-toes.

'Sorry,' she whispered and turned. 'I didn't mean to wake you up.'

'I wasn't sleeping.' Vanessa smiled mischievously.

Heidi gasped in mock exasperation, placing her hands over her breasts. Vanessa threw her head back and laughed.

Oh my God, you even look beautiful first thing in the morning.

'Can I take you out for breakfast?' Vanessa asked.

'Hmm, sounds like a plan,' Heidi replied as she sat on the edge of the bed.

Vanessa glanced at the clock on the bedside table. 'It's only seven o'clock, not many places will be open.

How about I make breakfast at my place,' she offered. 'What do you say?'

Heidi answered in a heartbeat. 'I say yay!'

'Do you mind if I take a quick shower?'

'Nope, feel free. You can even wear my dressing gown if you like.'

Vanessa eyed her gown on the back of the door. 'Would you be offended if I pass on this occasion? Pink's not really my colour. I'm more of a yellow sort of lady.'

'Okay, I'll let it go this once. Let me just use the toilet first,' Heidi said before walking to the bathroom.

Heidi returned to the bedroom minutes later and directed Vanessa to the shower. As she sat back on her bed she couldn't take the smile off her face. That was until her phone beeped and she read the message.

Everything is set to go.
Long live the centre lol

Dread tore into Heidi's heart as she realised that, in less than two hours, all of Berkley O'Neil's dirty little secrets would become public knowledge, and the woman she could hear singing happily in the bathroom would be caught right in the middle of it. It was too late to stop Simone now; hadn't she told her that it was the right thing to do?

Rather than working her mind into a frenzy, Heidi busied herself washing the few dishes cluttering up the small kitchen. By the time she'd packed away the last plate, Vanessa joined her.

'Penny for your thoughts?' Vanessa said, fiddling with the button on her shirt.

Heidi tossed aside the dishcloth. It was the moment of truth. 'Vanessa, we need to talk.'

Her words were met with a kiss. 'I don't want anything to spoil our day today. Look, I've even turned my phone off. I haven't done that since I first bought one.'

Heidi slipped her arms around Vanessa's waist. 'In that case, I'm one lucky lady.'

'No, I'm the lucky one. You are so beautiful,' Vanessa said in a moment of quiet contact; she stared at her with mesmerising eyes. They were laughing, even though her mouth wasn't, and her gaze sank deep into Heidi's soul, confusing her priorities—at least the professional ones.

'So are you,' Heidi said and welcomed her lips.

Vanessa's hands fell on the small of Heidi's back and she pulled her body against her own.

'Let's go back to bed?' she whispered in Vanessa's ear as Heidi virtually melted into her embrace.

***

After picking up a few things from the supermarket, and stopping for Nutella crepes and hot chocolate with whipped cream, it was midday before Vanessa and Heidi set off to her house. Vanessa was adamant about cooking her lunch, since they'd eaten breakfast out.

'Seriously, I wouldn't mind just having a toasted cheese sandwich, after filling up on the crepe,' Heidi insisted.

'I'm sure you wouldn't, but today you're my guest, so I'm cooking,' Vanessa retorted. 'Don't worry, I won't poison you for draining all of my energy. I couldn't go into work even if I wanted to.'

'It was worth it, wasn't it?' Heidi asked. Before everything blew up in her face, she needed to know that what they had shared meant something to Vanessa.

'You're damn right it was.' Vanessa grinned as she gave Heidi a sideward glance. 'Hey, what's with the serious face?'

Heidi took Vanessa's free hand and held it tight in her own. 'Nothing. I just want you to remember last night was something special.'

'I do, not forgetting this morning. Here we are,' she said pulling into her driveway. 'I hope Maggie hid all my sex toys.'

Heidi laughed. 'Maggie?'

'Maggie's a family friend. She's like a mother to me.'

'No competition then?' Heidi said as she looked out of the window at the size of Vanessa's house.

'Not unless you feel threatened by seventy-eight-year-old women.'

'That all depends. She might be a fit-looking pensioner.'

'Even if she was,' Vanessa planted a kiss on Heidi's lips, 'you'd still have nothing to worry about.'

Vanessa casually got out of the car, grabbed the shopping bags and led Heidi into the house. Inside was beautiful; elegant, but in an understated sort of way and not at all what Heidi had expected.

'You approve?' Vanessa asked.

'Are you crazy? What's there not to approve of?'

Vanessa's gaze followed Heidi's, as she looked around with wide eyes. 'What's the matter?'

'Nothing. It's just … I thought your house would be all marble floors and golden chandeliers,' Heidi said.

'Oh God, no! Even if I had a sheik's money I wouldn't sell out my sense of style like that.'

Impressed, Heidi's gaze roamed over the sweeping wooden staircase. The kitchen was spacious, *about the size of my flat give or take a few feet*, but true in keeping with the style of the rest of the house. It was charming and functional.

'Now, you can help me, but I'm still the head chef. I call the shots,' Vanessa said as they unpacked the ingredients.

Heidi had peeled potatoes, washed vegetables and poured nearly a bottle of wine by the time everything was cooking away on the stainless-steel hob.

The front door slammed shut and Vanessa and Heidi exchanged glances.

'Expecting someone?' Heidi asked.

Vanessa sighed. 'My niece.'

Just as the words left her lips, Kelli walked into the kitchen and stopped in her tracks. Her face was like that of a trapped animal at the sight of Heidi in Vanessa's kitchen.

'Hi, Kelli,' Heidi said lightly.

'Hey, Heidi,' Kelli said without hiding her shock. She turned and grimaced at Vanessa.

'What's wrong?' Vanessa asked.

'You! You just had to infiltrate the one place I can go to get away from you?' Kelli shouted.

'Kelli,' Vanessa started.

Kelli turned away from her and looked at Heidi. 'Not everyone falls for your charms, Vanessa. Some of us can see right through you.' With that she stormed out of the kitchen.

'See?' Vanessa said helplessly. 'You see what I have to put up with? What did I do wrong this time?'

'You didn't do anything. Let me see if she'll talk to me.' Heidi placed her glass of wine on the counter and went in search of Kelli. She found her sitting in the garden on a patio chair. 'Hey, are you okay?'

'No. No, I'm not. She even had to take you, Heidi. First, she tries to destroy the centre. Now she's taking you too, leaving me with no one to turn to.'

'Do you mind if I join you?' Heidi sat in a seat opposite Kelli, when Kelli gave a nonchalant shrug. 'I understand how all of this looks, but it's not what you think. We all got off on the wrong foot and I'm not blameless either. All of this could have been avoided if we'd acted using our heads instead of our emotions.'

'So you're saying you don't care if the centre closes?'

'Oh God, yes. Of course I do. I only wish I

would've dealt with things a bit better from my end. I'm not saying it's right, but your aunt and uncle run a business. Buying and knocking buildings down is what they do. I suppose if it wasn't their company, it would have been someone else one day. Change is inevitable. It's just that some people deal with it better than others.'

'But what about the doc—' she stopped.

'The documents you gave us were very helpful. There were many wrongdoings, which I hope will be put right because of your actions.'

'Did you tell Vanessa it was me?'

'No, and I never will.' They sat in silence for a few minutes and Heidi stared up at the blue cloudless sky waiting for Kelli to speak.

'Did she tell you about my mum?'

'Yes. This must be so painful for you both—'

'For us both?' Kellie snorted. 'She doesn't care. She won't even talk about her. It's like she never existed.'

'Please believe me when I tell you this: your aunt is hurting, deeply. Adults are a funny bunch of people. She thinks by her being strong, she's helping you. She thinks she'll be letting you down if she shows any sign of weakness.'

'She told you that?'

'She didn't need to. I can tell by her actions. It's not every day I get strong independent business women crying on my shoulder.'

'She cried?' Kelli asked incredulously.

'Until she fell asleep; I think she's leaving the ball

in your court. She's waiting for you to go to her.'

Kelli looked thoughtful. 'I've been horrible to her. I said I wished she was dead instead of my mum.'

'Grief makes us say things we'd never normally say to another person. We lash out because we want them to hurt as much as we do.'

'I can't believe my mum left me.'

'What your mum did, Kelli, it wasn't to hurt you. To the ones left behind, it can seem like a selfish act, but no one can know another person's pain. In the end, not even you could save her, so how do you think your aunt was supposed to?' Heidi deliberately compared Kelli to Vanessa to show her that they were in the same boat. 'She loved both of you very much and neither of you have any fault in her choices. Only she had the power to save herself, and she chose her way, sweetheart, not Vanessa's and not yours.'

Kelli looked over her shoulder. Vanessa had appeared in the doorway behind her while she was talking. They stared at each other for a long while.

'It's true. I miss her so much, Kelli. You're all I have left of her,' Vanessa admitted.

Kelli showed no aggression towards Vanessa. She was quiet, at peace. Suddenly she jumped up and ran into Vanessa's open arms.

'I'm sorry, Aunty Vanessa.'

'So am I,' Vanessa said, squeezing Kelli tighter.

Vanessa gave Heidi a grateful nod over Kelli's shoulder.

The sound of the doorbell ringing spoilt what was

a touching moment between aunt and niece.

'I'll get it,' Vanessa said, giving Kelli one last hug.

Kelli walked back outside and said to Heidi, 'I feel like such a bitch.'

'Things can only get better from here—'

'So are you two hooking up now?'

'We're ….' Heidi's cheeks flushed.

Kelli giggled. 'It's all right. I know the score.'

They both turned their heads towards the open door when they heard shouting in the house. Craig's voice boomed.

Oh shit. Heidi looked around the garden for an escape route. All she saw was high walls, which she might have been able to climb when she was ten, but not now. His voice drew nearer and her hands actually started to tremble. Whether it was through fear or the adrenaline pumping through her body, she didn't know.

The thought of Craig berating her in front of Vanessa and Kelli made her feel sick to her stomach.

'Where is she?' Craig's voice thundered.

Kelli jumped to her feet and stood frozen as Craig came out of the house, storming directly towards them.

'Oh shit, he knows, Heidi, he knows I'm gay. He's going to kill me,' Kelli said.

Heidi was beside her in seconds. 'You've got nothing to worry about. It's me he's after.'

Kelli looked puzzled. 'You?'

'Get the fuck out of my sister's house, or I swear to God, I won't be responsible for what I do to you,' Craig shouted as he strode into the garden, red-faced and panting.

Heidi backed away. She caught sight of Vanessa standing near the back door, surveying her with something akin to disbelief.

'Uncle Craig—'

'Shut it little girl!' He turned his attention back to Heidi. 'Get out! Out!'

His bulging temples were more frightening than the crazed look in his eyes. Heidi ran around him and towards Vanessa. As she reached her, Vanessa crossed her arms. The tears in her eyes said it all.

'Don't say anything, Heidi, just go.'

'I wanted to tell you this morning, but I couldn't. Not after last night,' Heidi said, praying Vanessa would understand.

'You should have told me before I made the biggest mistake of my life.'

'A mistake? You can't mean that. It's not true.'

'Isn't it? I wish I'd never laid eyes on you. Now do as my brother said, get the fuck out of my house.'

Blinking away the tears, Heidi brushed past her and left.

The flower of love was pruned before it even had the time to grow.

Chapter Thirty

Vanessa climbed into the bubble bath and let her body sink under the water. Alcohol hadn't worked at easing the tension in her body; she only hoped hot water and Epsom salts would do the job. She closed her eyes and tried to be mindful, but Heidi's betrayal rampaged through her head. They had made love all night and not once did Heidi so much as give an inkling about the bomb that was going to explode the following morning. Not once. Vanessa had spent the whole day trying to understand what kind of person Heidi was to be able to do that. Not even Vanessa could be that cold. To release private confidential papers on the internet made Vanessa feel personally violated. Despite her attempts at damage control, contracts had been cancelled, partnerships that she had built over the years wiped out in a matter of seconds, all because Heidi couldn't wait to destroy them. It sickened Vanessa to think she had let Heidi into her home while she had been laughing at her the whole time. Heidi may as well have taken a knife out of the drawer and stabbed her in the back.

Vanessa let her arms bob on top of the water. She slid her head under and held her breath until her lungs burnt from the lack of oxygen. If only she could stay under, then she wouldn't have to face the uphill battle of trying to fix Craig's fuck-ups. Whenever there were problems, it was always down to him; and now, the woman she cared so much about, and connected with, in a way Vanessa didn't think possible, had added her own crap to the mix.

Without opening her eyes, Vanessa sensed someone in the room. Instinctively, she pushed her head out of the water and snapped her eyes open to find Kelli standing there. She had been crying; a lot by the looks of it. Vanessa had done her best to shield her from Craig's rage by sending her to her room, but that didn't mean she didn't hear the barrage of abuse he hurled at Vanessa.

'Can we talk?' Kelli said.

'Of course we can. Do you want me to get out?'

'No, stay where you are,' she said sitting on the toilet seat.

'Okay, whenever you're ready.' Vanessa assumed Kelli wanted to talk about Lauren and she was more than ready to give her the support she needed.

'I wrote you a letter.' Kelli's jaw was tense. 'But it's best if I tell you in person.'

Vanessa waited.

'It's about some things I found in Craig's office.'

Vanessa frowned. Kelli hadn't been back to Craig's house since the funeral. 'In his office? When were you in his office?'

'The other day, when I made copies of all of his dodgy dealings with the local authorities.'

'Jesus, Kelli.' Vanessa jerked into a sitting position, pushing waves of water over the bath's edge. She was too shocked by what she had just heard to be concerned with the water or her nudity. 'Please tell me you weren't the one who gave Heidi the ammunition to ruin our company's name.'

Kelli's silence was her reply.

'Oh my God. Why, Kelli? Why would you do something like that?'

'Because what Uncle Craig was doing was wrong; didn't you always say we have to tell the truth?'

In one sentence, Kelli and Vanessa knew it. 'Well, yes, but ….'

Kelli raised her eyebrows. What Vanessa said next would either make her look like a woman of her word or a hypocrite. She couldn't risk Kelli thinking the latter.

'You should have spoken to me first.'

Kelli's eyes narrowed and she nodded in agreement.

How could Vanessa have expected Kelli to come to her with this when they'd barely said a decent word to each other in over a year?

Vanessa lay back down in the water, fast regretting leaving the wine bottle downstairs. 'Okay, I respect what you did. You made a mature decision and it was the right one. I'm proud of you.'

'But you're still angry at Heidi aren't you.'

'I don't want to talk about her.'

'You never want to talk about anything important, that's your problem—'

'I said I—'

'No, please hear me out. That's why I wanted you to stay in the bath. So you can't shut me down, or hide in your office or run off to work. I thought it was just me you did it to, like there was something wrong with me, but I can see now … you do it to everyone.'

Vanessa had never felt so vulnerable in her life, so exposed and to hear Kelli say such things tore at her heart. 'Kelli, I'm sorry. There's nothing wrong with you—'

'But there's something wrong with Heidi, right? I mean that's why you didn't stick up for her?'

'That's different. Heidi betrayed me, our company.'

'No, she didn't.' Kelli was on her feet. 'Don't you see, she just stood up against something that was wrong. She didn't have to. She could have walked away and just left the people at the centre to fend for themselves—'

'Like I did with you,' Vanessa said as she recognised her actions had been the opposite to Heidi's, and the people at the centre weren't even blood related. Hot tears mingled with the bath water on her cheeks.

'I wasn't exactly easy to help. I see that now. That's what I've learnt from people who truly care about each other. We can make mistakes, and if we learn from them, we get a second chance.'

'Is that what we have, Kelli? A second chance?'

Kelli nodded. 'And you can have one with Heidi as well. She loves you, and I know you feel the same—'

'Don't be silly, I've only sl—' she paused, 'known her a few weeks.'

'It doesn't matter. I knew I was in love after a few seconds.'

Vanessa's eyes widened. 'You're … in love? With

who?'

Kelli grinned. 'Someone I met at the centre.'

'I've missed out on so much with you, haven't I?'

'We both have, but I'm not going anywhere. I can't say the same about Heidi though.'

Vanessa gave a wry smile. 'Who'd have thought I'd have learnt a valuable life lesson from you today. Thank you, Kelli.'

'Thank Heidi. If it wasn't for her, we wouldn't even be speaking now.'

'You know what? I think you're right. Even I have to admit she has done some good.'

It was too late to do anything about the company's reputation. Besides, whatever Craig had coming to him, he well and truly deserved. Somehow, after the dust settled, she would rebuild her father's reputation with a company he would be proud of.

And Heidi? Vanessa would just have to wait and see what the future held for them.

Chapter Thirty-One

Heidi sat with her elbows on her desk, staring blankly out of the window. Since yesterday afternoon, her mind had been in a daze. Fear and anxiety hadn't left her. The fear came from seeing rage and hatred on Craig's face; the anxiety from the thought of never seeing Vanessa again. Heidi had always been able to switch moods if she was feeling down, but this one was different. Her decisions normally only affected her; but choosing to release the personal papers about Berkley O'Neil was more far-reaching. Why hadn't she stopped to think of the lasting damage it would do to a company Vanessa loved?

Thinking back, before they had become intimate, the least Heidi could have done was warn her, giving Vanessa a chance to prepare herself for the onslaught. However, she hadn't. Heidi's moral compass had lost its bearings. She had been selfish with the need to have any part of Vanessa that she was offering. Heidi was no better than Craig in that sense; her actions had been thoughtless.

Now Heidi was afraid; of the future and of the past; yesterday especially. The look of hatred in Vanessa's eyes told her there was no going back this time. If she wasn't so tired of all the ups and downs the past few weeks had presented, Heidi would have buried her face in her hands and cried.

Footsteps approached, then Harry's voice sounded as he poked his head around her door. 'Visitor.'

Heidi let out a frustrated breath. 'I told you I don't want to see anyone today.'

'Oh, I think you're going to want to see this person.' He grinned, baring all his teeth. 'She's hot!'

Heidi rolled her eyes as Harry moved aside and seconds later, like a vision from the heavens, Vanessa came into view. Dressed in leather skinny jeans and knee-high boots, she didn't look hot, she was sizzling. Heidi almost forgot to breathe as her eyes roamed the length of Vanessa's body.

'Can I come in?'

She's only come to remind me of what I could have had. 'What will you do if I say no?'

'Come in anyway.'

'You've just answered your own question then.'

Vanessa closed the door behind her. Neither woman spoke. Heidi decided that since Vanessa had come to see her, she could be the one to start off by telling Heidi what a bitch she had been.

'We need to talk,' Vanessa said.

'About?' Heidi asked.

Vanessa removed a hairband from her wrist and pulled her hair back in a ponytail. The slow motion of her action was distracting; making Heidi envisage what a turn on it had been having Vanessa's hair sway and caress her naked breasts.

'Yesterday.' Vanessa's tone was regretful, which

made Heidi think she might have got it all wrong, that Vanessa wasn't angry with her after all; that she understood why she had betrayed her trust, even if it wasn't completely altruistic.

'Which part of yesterday?' Heidi asked, testing the waters. 'Where your brother threatened to beat the shit out of me or when you told me I was the biggest mistake of your life?'

'Both.' Vanessa sat on the edge of the desk beside her. 'Things got out of hand. I'm sorry.'

'Did I just hear right. Are you apologising? To me?' Heidi said, still unable to tell if Vanessa was being sincere.

'I know what I said was—'

'Hurtful?'

Vanessa nodded.

'So why did you say it? You looked like you meant it.'

'I probably did in the heat of the moment. I feel different now.'

Surprise and elation spread through Heidi at the realisation she hadn't totally screwed things up with Vanessa, that there was still a chance to redeem herself.

'And what made you change your mind?'

'Kelli.'

'Kelli?' Heidi asked with an air of puzzlement.

Vanessa spread out her fingers and ran them along the top of her thighs. 'We had a heart to heart last night and let's just say she made me see sense.'

'I'd like to have been a fly on a wall listening to

that conversation.'

'Look.' Vanessa held her gaze. 'I'm not going to lie. I still think you went about things the wrong way.'

'I didn't have a choice.'

'You had plenty of choices, Heidi. We spent the night together.'

How could I forget?

'You had plenty of opportunities to discuss things with me.'

Damn, what do I say to that? 'I think we were a bit busy, don't you?'

'It's not a joke—'

'I'm aware of that, but if you hadn't put me in this position in the first place, none of this would have happened.'

'So you're saying I'm to blame?'

'No, what I'm saying is that whether you like it or not, your company hasn't exactly been above board with its business dealings, has it?'

'No, and I'm trying to fix it.' A smile played on Vanessa's lips. 'Which is why I'm here.'

Here goes. Now we're getting down to the truth.

'I want to call a truce.'

Heidi gave her an inquiring look. 'A truce?'

Vanessa's enigmatic smile lingered. 'I want you to take down your Facebook page and stop slagging my company off to the press.'

Heidi eyed her suspiciously. So that was her game, get her defences down, warm her up then try and bribe her. What would be the dangling carrot? *More great sex?*

'And what do I get in return?'

'I will personally guarantee you can stay in this building for six months, until I find you a new building. We'll also give you a healthy donation so the rent won't be a problem.'

Heidi sank back in her chair. She would rather have had the offer of sex. At least she knew Vanessa would actually follow through. 'Haven't we been down this road before? The last time you said that, your brother tried to blackmail me.'

Vanessa's expression was serious. *That's what she must look like in the boardroom. Sexy and dangerous.*

'You have my word,' Vanessa said, her eyes boring into Heidi's making it impossible to look away.

'And does Craig know about this "truce"?'

Vanessa broke her stare and lowered her eyes briefly to the floor. 'Not yet, no, but I'll talk to him. I'll make him see sense.'

And pigs will fly. But if Vanessa said she would ensure it would happen, Heidi was willing to let it go. She was tired of the uphill struggle which she knew they would eventually lose. 'In that case, you've got a deal.'

'Good. Let's shake on it.'

When Heidi took her hand, Vanessa pulled her to her feet and guided her between her legs. 'Now we've got business out the way.' Her sultry eyes roamed over Heidi's face and stopped on her mouth. 'We need to get personal.'

'Does that mean you're going to kiss me?'

'Do you want me to?

'Depends.'

'On?'

Fuelled by a sexual rush, Heidi wedged her leg between Vanessa's thighs. 'On what we're going to do afterwards.'

A low moan escaped Vanessa's lips as Heidi increased the pressure between her legs. 'Hmm, and what do you want to do?'

'Oh, I don't know,' Heidi said looping her arms around Vanessa's neck as she brought her face close, their mouths barely an inch apart. 'I thought we could take the day off—'

'Another one?' Vanessa drew back slightly. 'Are you trying to get me fired?'

'Hardly. You're the boss.'

'So I am,' Vanessa's arms slipped around Heidi's waist.

'Problem sorted?'

'It looks that way.'

Heidi bit her bottom lip. 'What are your thoughts on whipped cream?'

Vanessa laughed. 'Whipped cream? I'm willing to try anything once.'

'Good. 'Cause I've got a whole can going to waste at home.' Heidi gently brushed her mouth over Vanessa's lips.

'What are we waiting for?'

Before Heidi could answer, the door opened and Simone walked in. 'I've just got off—' She stopped in her tracks when she saw Heidi and Vanessa's embrace.

'Oh, sorry I should have knocked.'

Heidi's cheeks burnt as she jolted back and straightened her clothes. 'No, not at all. We were just … um ….'

'I think I'll leave you two to talk. I'll wait outside.' Vanessa winked at Heidi. 'Don't be too long.'

'I won't.'

Vanessa nodded at Simone as she passed her. When her footsteps receded down the hallway, Simone let out a sigh. 'I thought nothing was going on between you two.'

'Things changed.' Heidi smiled. 'Anyway, she's given us six months to find somewhere else and a donation to help pay the rent.'

'And you're happy with that?'

'Aren't you? My issue has never been about staying in this building. I was concerned that we'd never be able to find somewhere as cheap as this place.'

'So, shall I just tell everyone that all their hard work has been for nothing? Heidi's got her leg over with the sexy new landlord so we should all just throw in the towel.'

'I didn't say that, Sim—'

'I know what you're saying. Your heart was never in this fight from the beginning.'

'How can you say that?'

'Because it's true.'

'Sim—'

'It's okay. Really it is. You've got the girl and no doubt you'll get yourself a cushy job. This place will be a distant memory soon.'

'You couldn't be further from the truth. I'm leaving because I have to. I'm drowning, Sim. Can't you understand that? My involvement with Vanessa has got nothing to do with my decision. Even if I hadn't met her, I would have still left.'

'Have you slept with her?'

'What kind of question is that?'

'I take it that's a yes.'

'Drop it, Sim.'

'I'll only drop it,' a grin broke out on Simone's face and she started laughing, 'when you tell me what it's like to shag someone so goddam hot?'

'You bitch,' Heidi said playfully punching her shoulder. 'You really had me going then.'

'It wasn't exactly hard. Look, I know how tough this has all been on you and I'm glad you've met someone who makes you happy.'

'You are?'

'Of course I am. You're my best friend. You always will be, I hope.'

Heidi pulled her into an embrace. 'Always.'

'You'd better go and find her before she changes her mind.'

'Are you kidding? With what I've got in store for her, she wouldn't dare.'

***

'I don't think I'll ever look at whipped cream quite the

same way.' Vanessa slid her tongue across Heidi's erect nipple, taking the last squirt of white foam in her mouth.

'It's our secret.' Heidi inhaled a shaky breath as Vanessa's touch sent shivers throughout her body. She tried to recall a time when the tip of a woman's tongue gave her so much pleasure. *How about never!*

'Of course. I promise I won't share it with another soul.'

'I hope not,' Heidi said, praying that she meant it. The thought of Vanessa doing what they had been doing the last hour with someone else was more than she could bear.

'I need to take a shower, coming?' Vanessa asked.

Heidi loved how comfortable Vanessa felt in her small cramped apartment. 'Yes, but ….'

Vanessa frowned as she reached out and stroked Heidi's face. 'What's the matter?'

'I don't want to sound needy or anything,' Heidi said, twirling a strand of Vanessa's hair around her finger.

Vanessa looked at her quizzically. 'But?'

Heidi inhaled and exhaled slowly. 'Where … do we go from here? I mean us. Is it going to be a friends with benefits kind of thing?'

Vanessa sighed as she pushed herself into a sitting position. She took a pillow, positioned it over her chest and crossed her arms over it. The expression on her face told Heidi she was going to regret asking such a stupid question. *Why didn't I just keep my mouth shut? I always spoil everything with my need to know.* Not that it really mattered.

By ignoring what was staring her right in the face was only prolonging the inevitable. She cursed herself for even bringing the subject up.

'I'm not going to lie to you, Heidi, but I really don't know if I'm the settling down sort of person.'

'It's okay. I understand,' Heidi said shifting further under the covers, suddenly conscious of her nakedness. 'You need to spread your wings.'

Vanessa gently shook her head. 'It's not about sex. How can I explain this? I—'

'You don't have to.'

'Yes, I do. It's not personal.'

Here we go with the script everyone uses when they're letting someone down gently. How the hell can it not be personal when it's me she's rejecting?

'I love my work, every aspect of it. I know it sounds pathetic, but it consumes me to the point of distraction. The thing is, I don't know if I've got enough room in my heart for a relationship and work.'

Heidi stared at her, trying not to let her know that her world had been pulled from underneath her. 'Okay.'

'I've upset you now, haven't I?'

'No. I'd rather know where I stand,' she said feeling near to tears.

'You're a lovely person, Heidi—'

'Oh, please no. Do not roll out that tired old line. It's worse than the "it's not personal" bullshit. I get it. I'm a grown woman. You don't have to walk on eggshells around me. You enjoy being single. It makes you happy. Good for you, but it's not my idea of fun.

I'm not cut out for that sort of relationship; being second best. I've been that way all my life, always accepting things I didn't want because I didn't feel worthy enough.' Heidi spoke curtly as she brushed away the tears as they fell. 'But you know what? I know I'm worthy. I might not have lots of material things or money, but I've got my pride and nothing, and I mean nothing, will take that away.'

'I appreciate that but it doesn't change the way I feel, so it looks like we're at a stalemate.' Vanessa reached over and stroked Heidi's cheek. 'I'm going to miss you. I really am.'

Heidi's heart plummeted, as if she had just jumped off a cliff. 'Me too.'

There were a few moments of uncomfortable silence, in which neither woman knew what to say. They sat there looking everywhere but at each other.

'Would you mind getting dressed in the bathroom?' Heidi looked for an excuse to hide behind, no matter how flimsy. She couldn't bear to see her again, to say goodbye. 'I think I'm gonna have a nap.'

'Okay,' Vanessa said softly, before rolling off the bed and gathering her clothes together. Fifteen minutes later, the front door slammed shut, leaving Heidi in her own little world again.

Curling into a foetal position, she hugged Vanessa's pillow against her face, breathing in her perfume as if it was oxygen. *I asked and she told me the truth.* Was that how worthless Heidi was, that someone would choose work over her? She knew Vanessa hadn't meant to be cruel with her words, but that didn't make it any better. Her inner voice mocked her, telling her that she was worthless. Unwanted. Used. All the things that she hated, that made her feel weak, etched their way into her soul.

Rocking from side to side, hot tears rolled down her cheeks. Maybe she had aimed too high with Vanessa. Heidi had known from the start she was out of her league, but that didn't help ease the pain that seized her heart. She closed her mind to the image of them, barely an hour ago, making love.

Tomorrow she would have to go into work, face Simone and tell her that her dreams of starting something wonderful and new with Vanessa had been built on sand.

Pretty much like everything in my life.

Chapter Thirty-Two

Vanessa glanced at her watch for the third time in as many minutes. Craig was late, which was unusual for him, especially when the reason she wanted to meet him was so important to the company. She'd tried calling him on his phone, but it was switched off. Nine o'clock and still no sign of him. Vanessa decided to wait another ten minutes and if he was a no-show, she'd have to go in search for him, even if it meant traipsing all over London. She had to tell him about her plans for the centre. She only hoped Craig would see sense this time and realise they had much more to lose the longer they publicly fought with her charity.

An uneasy feeling passed over Vanessa again. In truth, she hadn't felt her normal self since she'd walked out of Heidi's apartment the day before. She had seen the hurt in Heidi's eyes when she had laid down the truth, but she hadn't been able to stop herself. The last thing Vanessa wanted was Heidi railroading her into something she didn't want. *But I do want her.* That was the problem. Only under her own terms. *Which are what exactly?* Vanessa honestly didn't know. It certainly wasn't friends with benefits as Heidi had thought. She wouldn't have that sort of relationship with anyone, regardless of how she felt about them. If she was going to enter into anything, even if it was short term, she would go all the way.

'Would you like another coffee?' The young waitress who had served her earlier appeared at her side.

Vanessa took a moment to consider as she looked down at her empty cup. 'No thanks, I'd best be off.'

Gathering her coat and bag, she left the café, looking in both directions before getting in her car. Annoyed with herself for feeling guilty about putting her needs first, she revved the engine more than necessary and sped off in the direction of her office. If she was going to get through the day, she had to stop thinking about Heidi and get on with things.

Walking through the doors of the reception area, an overwhelming sense of dread washed over her.

'Morning, Gina.'

'Morning.' Gina averted her gaze and shuffled a stack of papers on her desk. She looked morose, as though she was contemplating a subject she did not particularly enjoy. It was obvious Gina wanted to be anywhere other than where she was.

'Gina?'

'Yes?' she said, failing to keep her voice even.

'Have you seen Craig? He was supposed to meet me for breakfast but never showed up.'

'He's in the conference room,' she whispered.

'Who's he talking with? A new client?'

Gina's face paled. 'No, the board.'

'The board?' *I should be present during those meetings.* 'Do you know what they're discussing?'

Gina hesitated, looking about the office at her mute colleagues. 'I was taking minutes, but Craig told me to leave. They were discussing … you.'

Vanessa couldn't believe what she'd just heard. *Me?* Leaning over Gina's desk, Vanessa asked, in a softer tone, 'What were they saying that was so urgent that a meeting had to be called so early?'

'Craig is trying to oust you from the company. That's why they're all here. I'm so sorry; I wanted to call you to let you know, but he threatened to fire me if I said a word.'

That's just his style. Vanessa hurried along the corridor to the conference room. The doors were closed, obscuring the voices inside. She stood outside the door to collect herself. There was no point in going in like a bull in a china shop. She had to be composed. Articulate. Calm. All three things she didn't feel.

Taking a deep breath, Vanessa reached for the door handles and pressed them down at the same time. In one swift movement, she pushed the doors open and came face to face with an oval table of judges with her malevolent brother at the head, by the window.

'All those in favour?' Craig said as she strode in. His features froze. Vanessa gave him a knowing smile. *Yes, you little shit I know exactly what you're up to.* Now was the time to deal with him once and for all.

'Oh, I'm sorry. Am I imposing?' she asked, looking at the sea of blank faces that stared back at her. They clearly hadn't been expecting her. She could only imagine the yarn Craig had spun them. Instead of sitting, she strolled to the top of the table where Craig sat. He squirmed in his seat when she clamped her hand over his shoulder.

'You'll have to excuse me for being late. Craig led me to believe I was meeting him in a café, not the conference room, didn't you Craig?'

When Vanessa looked down at him, she could see the veins on his temple already bulging.

'I told you ... I thought ....' He loosened his tie, flustered.

'It's okay, you don't have to explain yourself. What matters is that we're all here now. I believe you were just about to take a vote. Does someone want to fill me in?'

Craig leered at her. 'If you must know, it was about you.' He gave a wolfish grin. 'We don't think your position here at the company is working out.'

'And why's that, Craig?'

He looked at her with disdain. 'Do you really need me to spell it out?'

'Actually, if you don't mind, I would.'

Craig cleared his throat and stood, his bulky figure towered over her. 'Since you've come on board, shares have fallen; and with this latest fiasco—'

'Would that be the fiasco of your making? The one where you were hell bent on evicting a charity, which has now led us to being investigated for bribery and—'

'Shut it Vanessa or—'

'Or what?' She looked up into his eyes. He didn't scare her anymore, and she wasn't going to back down. Not this time. This day had been a long time coming. 'Are you going to deck me in front of our board members?'

Craig gave an embarrassed laugh as he tried to make eye contact with the men and women around the table. Vanessa was relieved to see no one would meet his gaze.

'Did you really think you were going to come in here and make our board members complicit in your illegal practices?' Vanessa was bluffing; of course, she didn't actually know if they would get caught up in the investigation, but she was hoping they didn't know either. It wouldn't hurt to lead them along those lines.

'This has got nothing to do with me,' Craig shouted, totally losing his cool. 'This is all your fault, siding with that fucking dyke—'

'Yes, the manager happens to be a lesbian much like myself,' Vanessa said calmly. She would not take the bait and get into a screaming match with him. If she was going to win over the board members, she would have to do it with a sensible argument. They needed a reminder of what Berkley, O'Neil and Associates was about, not what Craig wanted them to believe. 'Is that why you have a problem with her? So not only will the company have the stigma of being corrupt, we'll add homophobic to the growing list.'

'What! Don't listen to her,' Craig said desperately. 'She's putting words into my mouth.'

'Our board members aren't fools. They worked for our father.' Vanessa leant on the table, addressing each of the board members individually as she spoke in a calm reassured voice. 'Believed in him as an honourable man, friend and businessman. They believed in his vision.'

Many of the heads nodded in agreement.

'Our business partners deserve what they bought into: growth and profit based on trust and moral decisions, not the destruction of lives for the sake of making more money.'

Vanessa gave Craig a sideward glance and could see his crimson face trembling.

'How dare you,' he shouted. 'We've made a forty-two percent profit in the last year alone thanks to my deals. What the hell have you done?'

'How about I tell you what I haven't done. I haven't cheated, bullied and bribed every official I've come into contact with and I haven't dragged this company's name through the mud. You have.' Vanessa turned her attention back to the people seated at the table. 'Ladies and gentlemen, my father built this company from nothing, using only moderate persuasion and sound business ethics. You know this. Now, because of the Young Minds Centre's unnecessary, imminent destruction, we are rapidly losing our reputation as a property company bent on the betterment of neighbourhoods. Have we forgotten what my father set out to achieve with this company?'

She could see their wheels turning, although they said nothing.

'If we demolish the Young Minds building, we will become public enemy number one,' she explained. 'Our name will be synonymous with bribes and corruption. It's professional suicide in my opinion.'

Craig was beside himself, clenching his fists in silence.

Now was the time to present the project that she and Brett had been working on throughout the night. It was the one she would have shown Craig had he bothered to show up. 'I have plans drawn up for a new, exciting complex of flats to be erected around and on top of the centre. We will renovate the centre and it will preserve our integrity, as well as bring in more profit than it would if we demolished the building. This is a win-win situation for us all and we can salvage what is left of our tarnished name. So vote if you must, but unlike Craig, I'm working towards garnering more respect for us. Respect builds bonds. Money is expendable. Our reputation is not.'

With that, Vanessa gave them a curt nod and walked out of the room. Reaching her office on unsteady legs, she hoped she had done enough to sway the board members' opinions, more for the company's sake than her own. *If they do side with him, do I really want to be involved in a company with Craig at the helm?*

Vanessa needed to do some serious soul-searching, otherwise, her happiness was in as much danger as the Young Minds Centre.

Chapter Thirty-Three

'I can't believe how stupid I was. What was I thinking, Sim?'

Heidi and Simone strolled through the local park. The sun shone and what should have been a great day, the start of a new beginning, had started out a dismal one. Simone had dragged Heidi to the park after finding her in the toilets in floods of tears. She had become overwhelmed by Vanessa's words. Vanessa's rejection still haunted her and stomped on her heart.

'You were thinking you'd found someone who was on your level. It happens to the best of us,' Simone said.

'But I should have known better. I'd read about her numerous flings in the paper. What made me think I was any different?'

'Because you are; it's her loss and if I'm being honest, you've made a lucky escape. Women like her don't understand anything about love.'

'I don't care about love, well I do.' Heidi said as they came to a standstill at a small man-made pond. 'I just didn't want to be treated like an unpaid prostitute.'

'I don't blame you. The least she could have done was leave you a few hundred for your services.'

Heidi laughed despite herself. It had been the right decision to get out in the fresh air instead of moping around in her office. She looked at a couple sat on a bench a few feet away. The young woman's arms were wrapped around a man's waist; her head rested on his shoulder. He said something to her and she giggled uncontrollably. Heidi felt a stab of jealousy when he turned his head and planted a kiss on her forehead.

That could have been us.

Simone followed her gaze, and snorted. 'Hey, dreamy, get your head out the clouds. They're most probably having an affair. No one looks that happy in real life.'

'I did. The short time it lasted anyway.'

Simone looped her arm through Heidi's and they started walking again. As they passed the couple, Heidi caught the woman's eyes and she could see happiness blazing in them. That was no affair. It was love.

'So, what are you going to do?' Simone asked, bringing Heidi's mind to a place where she didn't want it to be. *The future?* Heidi didn't even want to think about now, let alone tomorrow, next week or next month.

'Wait I suppose, and see if Vanessa follows through with her promise to get us an extension. After that, who knows?'

'Do you think that ogre of a brother of hers will agree?'

Heidi shrugged. 'Let's keep our fingers crossed.'

'I'm really sad about the way things have turned out.'

'About us having to leave the building?' Heidi inquired; her own heart heavy at the thought.

'Yeah, but mostly about you leaving. We've got so much history. It's not going to be the same going into a new office, with a new manager.'

They walked towards a bench placed near a children's play area and sat down.

'You know you could always take my place, keep the continuity going.'

'Me? A manager?' Simone said with laughter in her voice. 'Can you imagine?'

Heidi thought for a minute. Why shouldn't she? Everyone at the centre knew her and liked her, and Simone knew as much about the centre as Heidi did herself. There were times when Heidi thought Simone should have been the manager, such was her endless enthusiasm.

'Yes, I can. It would be good for the centre, keeping a familiar face through the transition. I'd think about it.'

'Okay. I will, under one condition.'

'What's that?'

'You put Vanessa out of your head and start being kind to yourself. You don't need her. You don't need anybody.'

Heidi bent over, picked a twig up from the ground and drew circles in the mud. 'I suppose.'

Heidi knew she would never be able to rid Vanessa from her heart completely. Not now. Not after the connection she had felt. Even if Vanessa didn't feel the same way, a trace of her would always be a part of Heidi.

'Are you all right?

'Yeah, I feel much better.' Heidi dropped the stick on the ground. 'I'm so tired. I need to sleep for a week.'

It may have been a bit drastic, but Heidi had spent the night sleeping on the lumpy, uncomfortable sofa. When she had lain in bed, the same one they had made love in, laughed in and connected in, memories had played on loop. There was no getting away from them. Even Vanessa's scent still remained, long after Heidi had frantically changed the bedding. It was if she had seeped into every area of her life and there was no getting away from it.

Heidi's plan was to move to a new apartment when she finally got a new job. Vanessa was only a minute part of her decision. She decided long into the night that if she was going to change, it would have to be in all areas of her life. If Heidi wanted a relationship, she was going to have to put herself out there. She wasn't going to find anyone by living like a hermit; and she was never going to be happy living in a cramped one-bedroom apartment. It was time to put her foot on the property ladder. Start taking control of her life, to be more like Vanessa—ruthless to the point of putting her needs first above all others.

Heidi was going to turn her life upside down and God help anyone who tried to stand in her way.

***

Heidi got out of bed feeling weary. No matter how many sheep she'd counted, sleep had remained elusive. She stripped off her clothes and made her way to the bathroom, deciding a shower was the way to go.

Stepping into the cubicle, Heidi let the hot, steamy water assault her body. *I wonder what Vanessa ... No stop it, focus on something else. Food. I'll order a take away. I'll get a curry since I missed out on the one Vanessa ... No, I said don't think about her.*

Heidi switched the shower off and grabbed a towel before drying herself in front of the mirror. She looked at her toned body from side to side and realised she'd lost a little weight lately. Her ribcage was noticeably prominent, which was not a good sign. It normally meant she was stressing more than usual. *It will be over soon. Then I won't have to worry about the centre ... or Vanessa.*

Heidi quickly dressed in a pair of jogging bottoms and a t-shirt and made her way to the living room. She couldn't remember the last time she pigged out in front of the TV. Grabbing the Indian menu from underneath the coffee table, she scanned the items.

They all look so good; I think I'll go for... Her phone rang. She ignored it. *Sod off. Hmmm the Vindaloo with...* Her phone rang again.

'Jesus Christ, can't I get a minute's peace?' *What if it's Amanda?* She dived for her phone and pressed it to her ear.

'Are you doing anything tonight?' Vanessa said.

Heidi's body reacted to her voice before her brain did. 'Sleeping.'

'It's only eight o'clock.'

Heidi exhaled loudly in a sigh. 'That's the beauty of living by yourself. You can do whatever you want.'

'There is that I suppose, but there's no fun

sleeping alone—'

'Did you call for a reason, Vanessa?'

'Yes … to invite you over—'

'I don't think so. I told you I'm not into friends with—'

'Whoa, you're getting ahead of yourself, aren't you? I have some news that I'd rather tell you in person.'

Heidi's heart sank. Those words usually meant the news was too hard to handle and had to be conveyed where a shoulder could be offered.

'Can't you tell me on the phone?' Heidi couldn't imagine driving all the way to Vanessa's house in a state of apprehension about the fate of the centre.

'No, believe me you're going to love it.'

Heidi took the towel off her head and dumped it beside her. 'I swear if this is just a guise to get me into bed, you're wasting your time.'

Vanessa laughed. 'Trust me, I won't come anywhere near you,' she lowered her voice, 'that is, unless you want me to.'

'Give me an hour,' Heidi said trying to convince herself the goosepimples that had erupted over her body had nothing to do with the thought of seeing Vanessa again.

'An hour? Are you coming via Edinburgh?'

'I've just got out the shower. I'm still wet.'

Vanessa laughed. 'Tease.'

Chapter Thirty-Four

When Heidi pulled up in her car outside Vanessa's house, Vanessa was waiting on the doorstep. Heidi's stomach fluttered and she willed herself to be strong. *Just listen to what she has to say then get out of there.* She unbuckled her seat belt. *And whatever you do, don't look in her eyes.*

The moment she stood beside Vanessa, all her plans fell apart. It happened when Vanessa placed her hand on Heidi's back to usher her inside.

'I like your hair curly,' Vanessa said eyeing Heidi's thick unruly hair. The hairdryer had turned it into a frizz ball. 'Very sexy.'

Heidi shot her a warning stare and Vanessa held up her hands as she laughed. 'Okay I get it, no touching, and no compliments.'

Heidi patted her hair down, suddenly conscious of it now. 'So, what's so important that I had to come here?'

'Champagne?'

'Am I going to need it?'

'Yes. To celebrate.' Vanessa popped the cork and poured the golden liquid into two tall champagne flutes. 'First, the bad news.'

'Oh God, I knew there was a catch.'

'This isn't going to affect you. Just me.' Vanessa handed her a glass and clinked it with her own. 'Craig resigned from the company today.'

Heidi almost choked on the bubbles in her mouth. She forced them down and looked at Vanessa in astonishment. 'That's not good news, that's brilliant news, isn't it?' she said taking another mouthful of Champagne. *It was worth coming over just to hear that.*

'Well, yes but my dad's upset seeing Craig's time at the company come to an end like this.' A flash of annoyance crossed Vanessa's features. 'Do you know what he did? He actually tried to get our board members to vote me out. Can you believe that?'

'The only thing I can't believe is that you're at all surprised. I'd put nothing past that man. Nothing. So, what's going to happen next?'

'It's now my duty to rebuild the company's name. And the good news for you—'

'What? What?' Heidi pressed.

'The centre is going to stay exactly where it is.'

Heidi's mouth dropped open. 'No! Seriously? Are you joking?' Heidi asked, in genuine disbelief.

The war was over. Heidi lunged forward and threw her arms around Vanessa, forgetting the non-touch rule; forgetting about everything except how wonderful Vanessa was. In the end, she had come through for them.

Heidi drew back, holding Vanessa at arm's length. 'How did you get them to change their minds then?'

'I presented a new solution. We're still going to build flats there, but around and on top of the centre. It's perfect, isn't it?' Vanessa said, obviously proud of what she'd accomplished.

'Genius,' Heidi said. 'Sheer genius!'

Heidi's phone pinged in her pocket but she ignored it. Vanessa gave her a questioning look. 'Aren't you going to check your messages?'

'Messages?' Heidi asked.

'You can answer it. I won't think you're rude, you know.'

Oh my God. Can you be more perceptive of me?

'Okay, only because you're insisting.' Heidi withdrew her phone from her pocket and scanned her messages. There was an email from Citizens Advice reminding her of her interview date the following week. She had been so caught up in the fight to save the centre that she'd forgotten all about it. But now that the centre was safe, it would be great to finally tell someone the truth.

'I have an interview for a job next week.'

'An interview? What about the centre?'

'As sad as I'll be to leave it, I really need a better-paying job,' Heidi said.

'Do you know anything about properties? I could always use a PR mastermind to rebrand the company,' Vanessa said in between sips of her drink. 'Just putting it out there.'

Heidi imagined working with Vanessa every day would be like having three Christmas' at once, but the torture of not being able to be with her dashed cold water on those thoughts.

'I'll keep that offer in mind.'

'I have another offer,' Vanessa said, as she slowly lowered her eyes with the intent of looking naughty.

I can't give in. I can't. 'And what would that be?'

'You could stay the night. I could cover your body with massage oil and rub you all over … We could drink champagne, then after …'

Heidi's breath caught in her throat as Vanessa took a step towards her. 'After?'

'We could have a hot steamy shower.'

The nearness of Vanessa's body flustered her and Heidi's heart leapt in response to Vanessa's suggestion. *Naked? In a shower?*

Heidi gulped at the heated desire in Vanessa's eyes and she slowly wrapped her arms around Vanessa's neck. If this was how good things were going to be between them, perhaps asking for the moon was a little overrated. She'd settle for whatever Vanessa was offering; as long as she was enjoying herself, why the hell not.

'How could I refuse an offer like that?'

'You can't,' Vanessa said.

Heidi's heart hammered in a frenzied rhythm as she settled her mouth on Vanessa's and kissed her long and hard, her tongue probing and searching every inch of her mouth.

'Just one thing,' Heidi said.

'What's that?' Vanessa asked breathlessly.

'Can we leave the massage until after the shower?'

Vanessa laughed. 'We can do whatever you like. The night is yours.'

The scent of vanilla permeated the bathroom from the candles Vanessa lit. She guided Heidi to the middle of the room, and tantalisingly slowly, began to remove Heidi's clothes. Sure, confident fingers unbuttoned Heidi's shirt and pushed it back over her shoulders before tossing it aside. Vanessa moved closer as her hands reached behind Heidi's back to expertly unclip her bra. Standing there exposed, Heidi drew in a deep breath when Vanessa's fingers gently swept over her erect nipples before searing a path down to her waist. Her jeans slid to the floor moments later, swiftly followed by her underwear. Keeping her eyes locked on Heidi's, Vanessa quickly undressed herself before taking Heidi's hand and leading her to the shower. Under darting pellets of water, Heidi flattened her back against the tiles, the cool surface causing goose pimples to explode over her skin as Vanessa's mouth covered her breast. Sucking, circling, teasing. Then, Vanessa's mouth was on Heidi's, hot and hungry, devouring her in a mutual assault. Heidi entwined her fingers in Vanessa's damp hair as Vanessa's mouth moved to her neck, nipping Heidi's throat with her teeth. Heidi's clit throbbed when Vanessa closed her eyes and bit her bottom lip as Heidi slid her hand between her legs. Vanessa was already wet and waiting.

Vanessa took a sharp breath as Heidi's fingers plunged deep inside her. Long lustful groans escaped Vanessa's lips as each thrust filled her. Still inside her, Heidi pressed Vanessa against the wall. Maintaining her thrusting rhythm, Heidi slowly knelt down. Water blurred her vision as she looked up into Vanessa's face, but she didn't care; she needed to see the sight of Vanessa's sexual hunger as she fused her mouth to Vanessa's most intimate nerve centre. At the probing of Heidi's tongue into Vanessa's molten release, Vanessa's body jerked uncontrollably, causing her to grip the back of Heidi's head. Vanessa grabbed fistfuls of Heidi's hair as Heidi slowly withdrew her fingers and clasped both hands firmly on Vanessa's behind to steady her. She pressed her hot tongue into Vanessa's entrance, bringing Vanessa ever closer to the moment she was now pleading for.

Heidi didn't remember when exactly, or how they exited the shower and went into Vanessa's bedroom, but they were now sprawled out on her enormous bed, as their water slick bodies writhed and grinded. Fingers probed and stroked, tongues teased and searched.

And much, much later, as their bodies vibrated with the strength of an earthquake, Heidi knew in her heart that no matter what the future held for them, she never wanted to be without Vanessa again.

Chapter Thirty-Five

They couldn't carry on like this, Vanessa decided, as she watched over Heidi as she slept. She was so beautiful, giving, loyal, warm, loving and as sexy as hell. Heidi was everything anyone could ever want *and so much more*. She would have to make up her mind to either accept the way she felt about her, allowing things to move forward or end it once and for all. The thought of never seeing Heidi again made her heart sink, but she knew if she couldn't, or wouldn't commit to her, the only solution would be to let her go. Heidi deserved better than to be messed around.

As usual, when Vanessa found herself wanting to avoid the inevitable, she opted to work. She needed some head space. Besides, she would never make a decision that was going to affect the rest of her life in the aftermath of a few hours of amazing sex.

Vanessa gently kissed Heidi's temple before easing herself out from underneath the covers. She dragged on a pair of jeans and a jumper before quietly letting herself out of the room. Glancing down the hallway, Vanessa noticed Kelli's light was still on under the door. She hadn't heard her come in; she only hoped that Kelli hadn't heard their lovemaking. The last thing Vanessa wanted was to embarrass her or make her feel uncomfortable. Nobody wanted to hear their aunt having sex.

Turning her desk lamp on, Vanessa settled on her chair with the full intention of working on the new proposal for the centre, yet every time she looked at the new design, her mind flooded with images of Heidi and the first time they had met. It seemed so long ago now; she could barely believe it had only been a matter of weeks.

Vanessa cocked her head when she heard a sound downstairs. She smiled to herself when faint footsteps caused the staircase to creek. Vanessa had been mistaken—Kelli wasn't upstairs after all; she was sneaking up to her room now. Although it was two in the morning, Vanessa decided to give her a break. As long as it wasn't the police bringing her home, she would give her some slack.

Right. Concentrate.

A loud click sounded down the hallway, but Vanessa decided against investigating it as she didn't want any more interruptions. She rolled out the plan and peered closely at it. Brett really had done a wonderful job of incorporating the centre. She knew Craig was livid at her new proposal; pretty much as she had expected, but with Kelli's vote in a few days, there was no way he could have reversed the board's decision. Now lost in her work, Vanessa was unaware of the impending danger. It was only when a burning smell invaded her nostrils that she quickly jumped to her feet.

Had she forgotten to put the fire guard up? With much speed, she ran downstairs to the living room, the smell much stronger now. She poked her head in, expecting to see a log on the floor burning, but there was nothing. Then she saw a faint grey cloud growing before her eyes. 'What the ….' She ran to the kitchen. Nothing was on—no pots on the hob, no sign of an electrical fire. Now convinced the smoke wasn't coming from inside, she walked to the front door and poked her head out, sniffing. Nothing. As she shut the door, she heard a strange noise coming from upstairs. Was Kelli burning something in her room? Vanessa bolted up the stairs, taking two steps at a time. As she rounded the corner, she froze. Paralysed in shock as waves of smoke engulfed her. It took a few seconds for her to comprehend what lay ahead. Fire. Climbing up the walls. Snaking its orange flamed body along the carpeted floor, all the way back to Kelli's room.

Kelli!

Thinking her name, Vanessa snapped out of her daze. She moved quickly towards Kelli's room, when suddenly an intense flame erupted, forcing her to jump back.

'Kelli! Kelli!' she screamed at the top of her lungs. 'Jump out the window. Can you hear me, jump out the window!'

Vanessa knew Kelli must have heard her. There was no way she couldn't have. Even as she thought this, Vanessa wondered why Heidi hadn't come out to see what the commotion was. An air of unreality permeated her as she spun round, ran to her bedroom and flung the door open. The stench of fumes was overpowering. Horrified, Vanessa watched the billows of smoke curl and crawl around the floor.

'Jesus! Heidi, wake up!' Vanessa screamed at the top of her voice as she raced to rouse her. 'Heidi? Heidi, can you hear me?'

But Heidi didn't respond. She was unconscious. Her head lolled from side to side as Vanessa shook her shoulders. The room, thick with smoke, barely had enough oxygen for Vanessa to breathe. Without thinking, Vanessa rolled Heidi's lifeless body into the cover like a cocoon and with all of her strength, dragged her off the bed and down the hallway, choking and retching as smoke filled her lungs. She couldn't afford to think about herself, her only consideration was getting Heidi outside. Jumping down a couple of stairs, she gripped the cover and pulled, trying her hardest not to hurt Heidi, yet at the same time, dragging her as fast as she could. Vanessa could now see shadows of flames flickering on the wall. At last, she was on the bottom step. With a mighty heave, she dragged Heidi the final few feet, her arms weakening with every pull. Vanessa made it to the door and, as she opened it, was filled with relief to see many of her neighbours swarming outside in their nightwear. Robert, her next-door neighbour, was at her side in seconds. He effortlessly pulled Heidi outside of the house.

'Here, let me see her.' A woman's authoritative voice came out of nowhere. 'It's okay, I'm a doctor.'

They both stepped aside as the doctor knelt down beside Heidi and began checking her vitals.

'Thank God you're all right. I called the fire

brigade,' Robert said. 'Is Maggie inside?'

'No. She's visiting friends.' Vanessa kept her eye on Heidi. 'Kelli had to get out the window—'

'Vanessa, I've been round the back.' His expression was forlorn. 'I didn't see Kelli. When I looked up all the windows were closed.'

Vanessa's body trembled and nausea overcame her as she glanced at her house and saw nothing but red angry flames. *Kelli!*

She imagined Kelli in her bedroom, slowly suffocating on the smoke. 'No I told her to jump out the window. She heard me, she must have. Please stay with her,' Vanessa's voice broke as she spoke to the doctor. Then without a second thought for her own life, she ran back into the house.

Chapter Thirty-Six

Vanessa awoke in the hospital cubicle and, in a panic, tore the oxygen mask from her face. Tears sprung to her eyes as the realisation of what had happened hit her with full force. Kelli was gone. Though her lungs burnt, she knew she couldn't stay in isolation, not knowing if Heidi was safe. Although the doctor had tried his best to persuade her to remain in bed for a few more hours, Vanessa had politely declined. She needed to be with Heidi, now more than ever. Someone had tried to kill them; that she was sure of. The stench of petrol still remained in her nostrils. If she hadn't woken up, they would both be dead now. It would only be a matter of time before the person responsible for lighting the fire realised that there had been survivors. What was to stop them from trying again?

Vanessa called the police and was informed that an officer was already on the way to the hospital. Feeling somewhat safer being surrounded by people as she waited outside Heidi's hospital room, she placed several calls to Kelli's mobile phone in a desperate hope that she would answer it, that somehow the impossible had become possible; but each call had gone straight through to voicemail.

Not wanting to believe the reality of the situation, in her mind, Vanessa had played out many different scenarios; one where Kelli could have escaped the inferno, or she was still hiding somewhere, unconscious but alive, but all scenarios led to the same conclusion. Not even seasoned fire fighters could have escaped that inferno without protective equipment and a water hose. Vanessa had racked her brain for hours, trying to remember if apart from Kelli's bedroom light being on, she'd heard any sound or movement. *Did she call out to me?*

The door to the room where Heidi was currently being monitored opened and a tall bearded doctor exited, still in conversation with a nurse. When he spotted Vanessa, he walked over.

'Can I see her?' Vanessa asked before he had a chance to speak.

He nodded. 'She's just coming round, but please, don't excite her too much. I'll be back in a few hours to check on her.'

Vanessa nodded her thanks and opened the door. For a few moments, she stood in the doorway, not knowing if she was strong enough to see Heidi yet. She stared at her still body and even from where Vanessa stood, she could see Heidi's flawless skin still had a few patches of soot. Having something to focus her mind on, Vanessa went into the toilet, took a handful of tissue and wet it before going to Heidi's side. Very gently, she wiped the dirt off her face, hoping that she wouldn't wake up yet; not until Vanessa's bloodshot eyes had shed their awful pinkness, but it was too late to hope. Heidi's eyes slowly opened. Upon seeing Vanessa, a faint smile played on her lips then disappeared, only to be replaced with a look of concern.

Heidi attempted to pull the oxygen mask from her mouth, but Vanessa gently restrained her arm.

'Don't try and talk,' she told her softly. 'I'm fine.'

Heidi's eyes bored into Vanessa's. Her voice was muffled beneath the mask. 'The house?'

Vanessa contemplated lying to her, but she didn't have the strength to carry through with it. However, she wouldn't mention the petrol. She would follow the doctor's instructions not to upset her. 'Gutted.'

Heidi closed her eyes briefly. When she opened them, she turned her head left and right, her gaze searching the room.

'Kelli?'

Vanessa couldn't answer. The words stuck in her throat. She couldn't bear to think again of the torturous vision she had of Kelli trapped in her room, waiting for Vanessa to save her. Just like she had when Lauren died, Vanessa had let her down. Again. 'She's gone, Heidi. Kelli's gone.'

Vanessa lowered her head and lay her face against Heidi's stomach. Heidi stroked her hair and, finally, the dam broke and Vanessa sobbed uncontrollably: For the time that had been wasted on arguing, for the time that they would no longer have together. Just when she thought that the final piece of the puzzle had slotted into place, it was sod's law to find out that wasn't the case after all. Vanessa had finally found the woman of her dreams, but at a price. *Why is there always a price? Why did I have to give up my niece as a sacrifice? How the hell is that fair?*

A knock at the door caused Vanessa to lift her head. A woman dressed in a dark blue suit appeared. For a moment, Vanessa thought she was a consultant, but the hardened look in her eyes told her she was most probably a police officer.

'Sorry to intrude,' she said, her eyes drifting from Heidi to Vanessa. 'Vanessa O'Neil?'

Vanessa nodded. She straightened, but entwined her hand with Heidi's.

'I'm Detective Sergeant Harrison from the London Met. I thought you'd like to know, the Fire Investigation Unit did a sweep of your house and no bodies were found.'

Vanessa's eyes widened. Her jaw literally dropped open. Had she just heard right. Kelli was nowhere to be found? She glanced down at Heidi for confirmation. Seeing the look of relief in her eyes confirmed it.

'Are they absolutely sure?' she asked.

'Yes. There was nobody else home,' she said. The officer stepped into the room and shut the door behind her. 'But from the report I read, it looks like the fire was set deliberately.'

'That's what I told your colleague,' Vanessa said, forgetting momentarily Heidi was listening. 'I knew it.'

Heidi looked up at her in confusion and Vanessa laid a reassuring hand on her shoulder. 'I'm sorry, I didn't want you to find out like this, but the house stank of petrol.'

'Ms O'Neil, is there anyone who would want to

hurt you?'

Vanessa looked at Heidi with horrid suspicion and Heidi shook her head.

The officer noticed the exchange between the women then advanced and sat down in one of the hard, plastic chairs. 'Look, if there's anything I should know, no matter how irrelevant.'

'It's just that I've been having a few problems with my niece.'

The detective took a small notepad from the side of her jacket. 'I see.'

'But we've sorted things out now—'

'And where is …?'

'Kelli.'

'Kelli now?'

Heidi squeezed her hand until it hurt. 'I don't think she would do something like this.'

The detective shrugged. 'I'd still like to have a word with her.'

'I don't know where she is. I thought she'd been caught in the fire.'

Heidi tore the mask from her face and rasped angrily, 'Do you really think Kelli would resort to killing us? She might have been angry, but she's no killer.'

The detective's phone rang and she gave them an apologetic glance before answering it. She listened for a few minutes before hanging up. 'I've just been informed a neighbour saw a black Bentley drive away a few minutes before the blaze. Do you know of anyone who drives that kind of car?'

Heidi and Vanessa exchanged shocked glances. Vanessa was so startled by the possibility of Craig's involvement that she could barely believe it, but that didn't mean she was going to let her disbelief stand in the way of justice. He had nearly killed them. 'Yes, I do. Craig O'Neil.'

'Craig O'Neil,' the detective said, writing the name down in a small notebook. Suddenly she looked up, wide-eyed. 'Isn't he—'

'Yes, detective. He's my brother.'

The detective rose. 'I'll bring him in for questioning. I'll keep you updated on our progress.'

'Thank you.'

After the officer left, Vanessa dropped onto the seat she had just vacated. She ran a nervous hand through her hair. 'That bastard. That dirty rotten bastard. Not even I thought he'd stoop this low.'

'I'm sorry,' Heidi said weakly.

Vanessa was on her feet again, leaning over Heidi and kissing her forehead. 'What are you apologising for?'

'If it wasn't for me and that centre, none of this would have happened.'

'And I would never have met the ....' She paused for a moment. The timing still didn't feel right. Not under such dire circumstances. 'You.'

Vanessa didn't miss the look of disappointment in Heidi's eyes. She would tell her the words she wanted to hear soon. Just not today.

Chapter Thirty-Seven

'Hey, Heidi.' A familiar voice filtered into Heidi's head. She opened her eyes and looked straight into Kelli's gaze. Alive, so very alive and well. She stood next to Vanessa, both beaming and holding flowers and chocolates.

'How're you feeling?' Kelli asked.

'Better for seeing you.'

'I'm sorry I scared you like that. Christina was meant to drop me home after the party but I decided to crash at her place,' she said, her pale cheeks suddenly flushing.

'Thank God you did,' Vanessa said, putting her arm around Kelli's shoulders and giving her a quick squeeze.

'Knock, knock.' A detective appeared in the open doorway.

'Detective,' Vanessa said warmly. 'I didn't expect to see you again so soon.'

'I was visiting someone so I thought I'd bring the news to you in person. We arrested your brother and he's been charged.' She gave a wry smile. 'He attended the Queen Elizabeth Hospital shortly after the fire with second degree burns.'

'I just can't believe it!' Kelli exclaimed. 'What a bastard!'

'Kelli,' Vanessa reprimanded.

'What? He tried to kill his own sister. The man is insane,' Kelli insisted.

The detective ignored Kelli's outburst and continued, 'Whatever he is, he felt bad enough to confess to starting the fire. He apparently did it in a drunken rage because you took away his job. He's been ranting non-stop and, to be honest, he isn't really making that much sense. Because of the premeditated nature of the crime, he'll be remanded without bail until his trial. At least you can sleep soundly at night, knowing he's safely behind bars.'

When they were alone again, Kelli sat on the edge of the bed. 'Why don't you come and stay with us when you're discharged.'

Heidi looked over at Vanessa and was shocked to see her nodding in agreement. If she were being truthful, Heidi didn't want to be alone. She was still traumatised by what Craig had done. She shuddered to think that if Vanessa hadn't been working in her office, they probably would have both been dead now. Knowing how close the end had nearly come, put life into perspective.

'Um, yes, I suppose I could for a short while. Until I get back on my feet.'

'Yeah, yeah,' Kelli said. 'You two make me laugh. Why can't you just admit you're crazy about each other?'

Heat rushed to Heidi's cheeks, but she remained silent. With how she felt about Vanessa, 'crazy' just didn't go far enough.

Kelli pecked Heidi's cheek and got to her feet.

'Anyway, I'll see you guys later. We're going to the cinema.'

'When you say we, I take it you mean you're going with Christina?' Heidi asked.

It was Kelli's turn to blush. 'Uh-huh.'

Heidi laughed at her bashful expression. 'Tell her I said hello.'

'Will do,' she replied before disappearing out of the door.

'It's so good to see Kelli happy again,' Vanessa said as she came to stand beside Heidi. She took her hands in her own. 'It seems we've both struck gold.'

Heidi feigned ignorance. 'How so?'

'Didn't you hear what Kelli said? I'm crazy about you. In fact ….' Vanessa bent down and whispered three words into Heidi's ear.

Heidi pulled Vanessa closer and planted a kiss on her lips. She was grateful the nurse had taken the heart monitor away, because it would have exploded for sure. It was ironic, Heidi reasoned, how one O'Neil had nearly killed her with hatred and the other with love.

Epilogue

Heidi sat back in her seat and looked around her spacious office, relieved there wasn't one thing out of place. There was enough room for everything to be stored away. She glanced at the framed picture of Vanessa on her desk, and her heart swelled the way it always did whenever she saw her. Several months ago, Vanessa had appointed Heidi as the Head of Public Relations at her new chain of counselling services that worked closely with places like the Young Minds Centre. It didn't take much to convince Heidi to join the company; after all, Vanessa's legacy would one day be left in the hands of the two children they planned to adopt after their Christmas wedding.

Heidi still couldn't believe how much her life had changed and, for the first time ever, in a good way. She was still in the throes of the honeymoon period with Vanessa and thought it would never end. Every day was like a new beginning. She knew it sounded clichéd, but until now, she'd never known love could be so deep and rewarding.

Kelli had discovered this as well. Not because of Heidi and Vanessa, but through her love for Christina. They'd been in a relationship for well over eight months and it looked like they had a bright and happy future together. Not only that, but they made such a cute couple.

Her phone rang and Simone's name flashed up on the small screen. Even though they no longer worked in the same building, they still managed to have their morning gossip session before work swamped them. Simone was the new manager of Young Minds and Heidi was proud to say she was doing a fantastic job running the place.

Heidi connected their call and before she could get a word in, Simone said, 'I just listened to your message about Craig. A five-year prison sentence really isn't long enough for what he did. He could have killed you both.'

'I know, but I'm glad it's all over with. Hopefully when he gets out, he'll take the money he received from selling his share of the company to Vanessa and retire in Timbuktu.'

'I wouldn't wish his presence on any country.'

'You never know. A few years in prison might be the making of him.'

Simone snorted. 'Yeah, if you believe in miracles.'

Heidi looked around the office, then down at the picture of Vanessa and herself embracing one another. Yes, she did believe in miracles. After all, she was living one herself.

Printed in Great Britain
by Amazon